RETURN TO ORPHALESE

Also by Philippe Souchet

Published by Les Eclosions Asynchrones

Incarnations, *a novel, 2011*

Return to Orphalese, *a novel, 2016*

The feed of the sybils, *poetry, 2017*

Under the walls of Time Eaters, *poetry, 2020*

Visit our website :
http ://www.eclosions-asynchrones.com

On Facebook : facebook.com/LesEclosionsAsynchrones

On Twitter : @EclosionsAsync

ISBN 978-2-9556679-4-1

PHILIPPE SOUCHET

RETURN TO ORPHALESE

a novel

*translated from French
by the author*

LES ECLOSIONS ASYNCHRONES

"O Mist, my sister, much did I love the world, and the
    world loved me,
For all my smiles were upon her lips, and all her tears
    were in my eyes.
Yet there was between us a gulf of silence which she
    would not abridge
And I could not overstep.

"O Mist, my sister, my deathless sister Mist,
I sang the ancient songs unto my little children,
And they listened, and there was wondering upon their
    face ;
But tomorrow perchance they will forget the song,
And I know not to whom the wind will carry the song.
And though it was not mine own, yet it came to my
    heart
And dwelt for a moment upon my lips.

"O Mist, my sister, though all this came to pass,
I am at peace.
It was enough to sing to those already born.
And though the singing is indeed not mine,
Yet it is of my heart's deepest desire."

Khalil Gibran, The Garden of the Prophet

Foreword

ORPHALESE is the name of a city, a mythical city invented by Khalil Gibran to serve as a setting for the message of *The Prophet*, his major work, and by far the best known.

This small text of about one hundred pages, both a collection of poetry and a mystical initiation, is considered perfect, and its immense popular success, uninterrupted since its first publication in 1923, is the perpetually renewed proof of this. Indeed, one cannot deny its unequalled spiritual significance in a contemporary work, by the beauty of its language and the universality of the chosen themes (love, marriage, children, freedom, pain...). A total of twenty-six poems, or hymns in the biblical sense, or chants in the Homeric sense, for the comparisons here are of this order, which deal with all the fundamental aspects of the dialogue between man and the divine.

Khalil Gibran called *The Prophet* a "strange little book", for he himself could not understand the magic it exerted on its readers, despite the many years he had spent perfecting every word and illustration.

How dare, and above all why, to add one iota to this monument of wisdom ? It was simply unthinkable, and the author of this book did not even try. However, it seemed to him that other themes, perhaps darker and more current (pollution, depletion of resources) or just as timeless (war, creation, writing) could be tackled by reusing the city of Gibran as an enchanting setting.

Nor is there any question of imitating the poet's literary style, an illuminated language tinged with archaisms, reminiscent of the ancient words of papyri and codices. Here we prefer to deliver a romantic tale, no doubt less ambitious, but more likely to develop a plot. This warning, more than necessary, having been made, here are some elements that supported the work of the editor.

He has used a few known landmarks to help him build his thoughts, which will probably appear randomly in the following pages.

The first step was to be guided by the play of sounds. In Orphalese, one can hear "Orpheus" and "Ephesus" , which leads to ancient Greece and Turkey, not far from Lebanon and Gibran's Syria. The present narrative has thus been inspired by the turbulent context of Mediterranean history, at a time when, a thousand years before Christ, the Greeks invaded all the shores of the sea, destroying among others the Minoan civilization in Crete, and establishing multiple colonies in Minor Asia. Inspired only, however, because this is not a historical novel but a fable, in a world as imaginary as that of "The Prophet " .

In French, one can also hear "or" *(gold)* and "falaise" *(cliff)*, and see a steep rocky coast, a chalk wall set ablaze by the rising sun, a ship reducing sail as it approaches the harbour.

The images are already scrolling, here is the set of our tale !

Another idea was to understand how the original word of a messianic prophet can be distorted or lost after his disappearance, despite the best will of his followers, who cannot fight against the abrasive effects of time and the dissolution of the original intention in the multitude. Moreover, what direct impact did the Prophet have on his closest companions ? How did they share and understand his teaching ? How did they survive his absence ?

These are some of the questions that served as a common thread throughout the writing of this book, always walking in the shadow of Gibran and remaining faithful to his Lebanese origins, which combined Christian (Maronite) and Muslim (Sufi) cultures, which in the present context is of particular importance.

A new little book, then, which has no other ambition than to tell a nice adventure by exploring a little further a universe created by another, most inspired poet, federator of two cultures that are wrongly considered as antagonistic.

This story begins twenty years after the disappearance of the prophet Almustafa, the Chosen and Beloved, a noon unto his own day...

O Master, how shall I speak to them ? I who had come so they might speak to me about you, behold, they urge me to hear your word through my mouth. They want me to remember everything you said when I was by your side !

And what would I tell them ? What have I learned from you ? How can I tell the compassion in your eyes and the warmth in your voice ? And how would the filter of memory not tarnish your message ?

You who made the most difficult concepts so simple, who found the images that everyone understood...

Now I understand better your concern, when you told us not to learn your teachings word for word, but rather to capture their essence, so that we could better render them with our hearts. "Only the heart," you said, "will get you through all the barriers of misunderstanding."

You left me alone, Master, and I forgot everything.

Part I

Almitra

IT wasn't until several minutes after a man on board had shouted "Land, ho !" that Youssef, standing at the bow of the ship, could finally see the white line of the shoreline thickening on the horizon. It was a miracle, after several days on the high seas which had sorely tested his insides. He wondered if the sailors really had exceptional eyes, or if some sixth sense had developed in them that made them feel the coast before they even saw it.

However, the good news meant the end of his endless odyssey, and that he would finally be able to put down his bag for a while, and perhaps even forever, if the destination of his journey was what he had hoped for.

The old man had the makings of a great traveller, or even a nomad who no longer knew his home port. His long white locks, curled up and stuck together by the salt, were sent from all sides by gusts of wind, and his beard, left without maintenance for years, gnawed at an annealed face, etched back and forth by all the paths he travelled. And yet, behind the bushy eyebrows, fiery blooms of fire were beading, and the liveliness of his eyes denounced an invincible optimism and energy. He approached the rail, as if to accelerate the speed of the ship and anticipate the moment when the goal of his journey would emerge from limbo.

At last the white city appeared at the turn of a last chalk wall, suddenly offering its splendours to the astonished travellers. Wedged between the ocean and the mountains, one could immediately feel that it had struggled to settle in this inconvenient place. Unwelcome, repelled by the forces of nature, it had nevertheless spread out over the centuries, gradually and pugnantly throwing its houses against the foothills, and its piers against the waves.

From the deck, Youssef could see majestic buildings protruding from the others, sending towers and colonnades towards the heavens. Palaces, temples, opulent villas, watchtowers, had over time given Orphalese a reputation of majesty, which had spread far beyond the country.

Orphalese ! The city of dawn, the cradle of the origins that had hosted the retreat of the Prophet, and accompanied his illumination ; the one that the great man spoke of only with a wet eye and a trembling voice.

The disciple, coming for the first time to this mythical place, wanted to find the traces of the presence of his master in the tortuous alleys crushed by the sun. What would remain of him, more than twenty years later ? And in the hills that overlooked the high quarters, at the bottom of the bay, were the hundred-year-old cedars still repeating his first teachings scattered by the wind ?

Having been over sixty for quite some time, Youssef had reached the respectable age where time flies faster than one would like. He had felt the urgency to write down the life and words of the man loved and revered among all, Almustafa, the Prophet, whom he had followed on all the shores of the sea, collecting every word that fell from his mouth like a precious stone destined to embellish the heritage of humanity.

"It is market day, it seems, said a sailor with a happy face. We are going to be welcomed like heroes, returning from distant lands with arms full of gifts !"

THE market of Orphalese was known to be one of the busiest in the country, with some of the most exotic foodstuffs brought in from remote areas with unpronounceable names by caravans that braved deserts, jungles and mountains year-round.

Once a week, it would spread his stalls with multicoloured hangings over most of the city, overflowing squares in the main thoroughfares, insinuating himself into the streets, then climbing up the hillside, up the steep stairs, into the almost inaccessible alleys where the least shining vendors were relegated.

An elderly lady with a haughty port already walked lightly through the alleys. The only marks on her face seemed to have been left by laughter rather than by time, so cheerful did she look, and accompanied every word she distributed with open and frank smiles.

She was the queen of this place, and everyone knew her, called her, hailed her, wanted to draw her footsteps with a thousand attentions.

Watermelons, eggplants, breads, fishes, baskets of olives, handfuls of spices, stretched out at his approach and punctuated his passage with joyful explosions of colours, smells and words of love.

She, a goddess with light feet, descended among men for a short moment, gave them her time. She sniffed, felt, tasted, appreciated, thanked and complimented. Then the crowd of her admirers, who accompanied her everywhere, kept getting bigger and bigger, men and women, young and old, merchants and passers-by. They repeated his name over and over again, in every tone, like an incantation : "Almitra ! Almitra !" .

And the tumult came towards Youssef, and the clamour came to his ears. When the name was spoken, the disciple stopped in the middle of the road and, incredulous, looked at the woman. She, now a few steps away, saw him and froze. Suddenly there was silence, and the people wondered who this stranger, this beggar, who was disturbing Almitra, was. She spoke first :

"A long time ago I knew a man who looked like you, old man. He lived among us for a time."

"A long time ago," replied Youssef, "I knew a man who sometimes pronounced your name, Madam. Each time, there was sunshine in his voice."

"If it was the same man, the light was coming out of his mouth every time he was speaking."

"So it's Almustafa we're both talking about, and which I had the joy of listening to long after you ! "

A new smile, even more radiant, lit up Almitra's face. "Finally !" she whispered. She approached the disciple and took his hand. The onlookers were reassured by her new disposition towards the unknown foreigner and let the strange couple go away without further disturbance.

"Brother, I've been waiting for news for so many years ! How did he disappear ? Did he suffer ?"

"I confess that I have lived through this ordeal from afar, and I prefer to erase it from my memory to keep only the good times we spent together..."

"How would you like to come and tell me about your adventures with the Master, one day soon ? I'm so eager to know how his last years went."

"I will do so with great pleasure, and I would like you to tell me about his youth as well. But first I must find a place to sleep tonight, and if possible a house where I can settle down for the next few weeks..."

"I can do nothing for you, alas, for there are three of us in my house, and our walls are already too narrow. But there's a tavern, over there, by the west gate. You'll certainly find someone there to help you..."

To thank him, the old man bent down to kiss her hand. She burst out with a charming laugh.

"How will I find you ?," he said, straightening up.

"Give my name to anyone in town, and they'll point you to my house... "

YOUSSEF arrived in front of the inn indicated by Al-mitra. A stout man was unloading a cart full of amphorae and carrying them into the establishment. Inside, the smells of food and wine popped into the traveller's face as he made his way through the crowds of people gathered around the counter. In the smoke and commotion of the guests, he looked for a free corner of the table, and slumped down heavily. Nothing would make him move from here until he had swallowed a real meal from solid earth. Meat in sauce, perhaps, which would finally fill the bottomless hollow that the unspeakable sailor's fricots had placed in his old belly, crossing after crossing.

The inn had to be famous all over the city, for the crowd was truly astonishing.

Not far away, he recognized the seaman who commanded the ship by which he had arrived. He turned his ear, trying to pick up bits of the conversation :

"So, Captain, what news from the wide world ?"

"Well, it seems it always turns upside down. No one remembers when or why this war began, but I can tell you it's not going to end anytime soon. As far as I can understand, the cities in conflict lose colonies and islands in turn, then reconquer them shortly afterwards, so that the borders, while in perpetual motion, are always more or less the same ! In any case for us, merchant ships, it is better not to choose a side, because you never know in which waters you are sailing ... I always have several flags in the holds, and my sailors have become unbeatable, in the event of a boarding, for changing colours at the last minute !"

"It's still a dangerous game," said one of the customers at a nearby table. "It's going to end badly one of these days !"

"You're right, my friend," sighed the captain. "I spoke to death more than once, and I can't count the lost shipments. Not to mention the pirates ! No really, maritime trade has become impossible these days. Besides, I can't explain how your city has stayed away from battle all these years !"

"It's a war for control of the seas," said a third guest, "while we do business on land. Our waters are far from the great trade routes. And we have no riches that the rulers of this world could covet...

"Consider yourself lucky," the captain said with a pout full of doubt. "I've seen many cities razed to the ground for no reason, by the simple whim of a capricious low-ranking officer."

His eyes blurred as he siped slowly.

"Still, we sometimes see large warships passing by, said the first customer. They're full of soldiers. You can see their helmets and armor gleaming in the sun. Clever who could tell which side they're on and where they're going... But so far, they have never turned their bow to Orphalese, praise be to God."

The fat man unloading the amphorae at the entrance of the inn had finished his work. Youssef saw him being paid his dues by the tavernkeeper, looking for a free place in the middle of the crowd, and displaying a smile of victory as he looked in his direction. In spite of his stoutness, he managed to sneak up to the old traveller, and sat down heavily at his side, a full jug in his hand.

"I'm not used to imposing myself," shouted the new-comer, still red from his efforts, to cover the surrounding crowd. "But on market days, we don't have much choice. Please accept this offering as a token of my good will."

And he put the jug noisily on the table. As if by magic, two cups appeared in his other hand, which filled before Youssef could say anything.

"I am a wine merchant, you see, and this is my production ; you will tell me about it !"

The two men toasted without any other form of ceremony, and the old man soon felt a gentle warmth flooding into his aching joints. Time flies as fast as the jugs when in good company, and they went off in lively and jovial conversation without seeing the hours pass.

This unexpected introduction, this instant familiarity, had put Youssef at ease, and he decided to share his immediate concerns with his new lifelong friend :

"I've just arrived, by this morning's boat, and I'm looking for a place to stay in town for a while. I've been assured that by coming here, I would easily find accommodation for a few nights, or even for several weeks. Do you have any connections that could help me ?"

"I don't think it's easy to find ! The city is packed, and the places are expensive !"

"Of course, you've guessed that, besides, I don't have much money..."

The wine merchant scratched his head for a moment, then snapped his tongue with a grimace :

"I've got an old shack on top of the cliff," he said, "an abandoned shepherd's cottage, but I warn you, it's far from luxurious. Moreover, it hasn't been lived in for years, and it must certainly be in a miserable state."

"That's all right, I've never really had a home of my own. It would already be a great improvement in my condition !"

"From the road that leads to the sea, at the exit of the town, there is a small path that goes up to the heights, and that runs along the coastline. Follow it for an hour, and you will come across the house. It's really very isolated, doesn't it frighten you ?"

"On the contrary, it will be perfect, I'm not very worldly if you hadn't noticed... How much do you want for it ?"

"Don't worry about that, no one will miss it, as I told you. Wait till you see it !"

The two men sealed their agreement with a frank handshake, and Youssef took his pack to begin the last part of his journey. So far, his stay had been very auspicious !

PRESSED by his business, the wine merchant had no time to accompany the old disciple. He left him at the bottom of the path that climbed up the hillside, telling him to stop at the first house he found, at the top of the cliff.

His baggage was meager, but after an hour of uneasy walking on steep, rocky paths, he began to saw his shoulder off deeply. So he was happy to finally find the shepherd's hut at the indicated place.

When he entered the shack, Youssef knew that he had not been lied to, because its layout was really very simple, and even very severe. A single window, but overlooking the sea, a thin straw mattress, a shaky wooden table and two stools on a dirt floor, one could hardly do less ! This did not bother the old man, who had seen others in his per-egrinations. On the contrary, he was determined to devote himself entirely to his great work, and not to be diverted by the artifices of modern comfort, which soften the soul and divert it from its primary goals.

After putting his few belongings on the pallet, and walking around his new estate in three steps, he stood on the doorstep for a long time, admiring the grandiose scenery that opened up before him. Those high, desolate, wind-battered cliffs, those emerald waters foaming endlessly, those seabirds asking loudly which intruder had come to get lost among them, all this would be his for the months, and perhaps years to come.

The city was far away, and could not be guessed. The path that had led him here disappeared at the bend in the terrain, and Youssef knew that very few would take it from now on.

Here, the incessant wind did not allow the trees to take root. Only a few tufts of rough, yellow, hard to hurt grass, cooked by the salt and the sun, clung here and there to the rock.

This solitude also suited the old man, who saw it as an atmosphere conducive to work and introspection. For it was within himself, in his heart and his memories, that he would look for the words to write. Not in the bustle of the world and its trivial affairs...

Back in the house, Youssef set up his study area. He pushed the table under the window, to take advantage of all the light that the day could give him, and unpacked his equipment. Two calamuses, a scraper, black ink for writing, red ink for correcting, and a bundle of paper. There would always be time to buy some in town if they ran out.

When everything was ready, he sat facing the window, calamus in hand, and let his gaze wander across the azure sky...

Almitra's prediction had turned out to be correct : the first person Youssef met was able to show him the way to her house.

The face of the queen of the market lit up when she found out who was knocking at her door, and the disciple was invited to share a modest dinner. He entered the house without being begged, and discovered an interior which, although imbued with great simplicity, showed a definite taste for harmony and beauty. The furniture, few in number, had clean lines, and everywhere flowers and candles delighted the senses.

In a corner of the room, next to the hearth where a fire had to be kept burning all year round, an old body was curled up in a wooden armchair between two high armrests. A woman was laying there, white and tortured like the cliffs, her eyes washed out by the years, staring obstinately at the flame. The thin slit of her mouth without lips was barely moving, letting out a complaint, an imperceptible rumble, which never ended.

"Who is it ?" asked Youssef.

"My husband's mother, Nedjma," answered Almitra. "She's been through many dramas during her long life, so much so that one day her reason remained trapped in a corner of her mind, the key to which we have never found."

"So you are married ? I had understood, according to

Almustafa, that this would never happen !" Youssef smiled.

The jest did not make his host laugh.

"This is one of the ordeals we went through toge-ther," she said."Adel, my husband, was a fisherman. Like his father before him, and his father's father, and as far as the memory of men can go. And like his father before him, seven years ago, he died at sea, during a campaign that was longer and later than usual."

A long, gloomy lament rose from the chair. Unsurpri-singly, the old Nedjma was not losing any of the conversa-tions under her roof, and Almitra's account had awakened the pain of a mother and a wife who, for a long time, and until her last breath, would remain locked in mourning.

Youssef was no longer smiling. He had not imagined, under Almitra's cheerful and debonair airs, that she and her family had gone through so much suffering.

Nedjma's complaint soon turned into an intelligible speech :

"So it is with our sad existences : our men go to distant waters to face dangers of all kinds while we, poor seafarers' wives, we mothers, we wives, can only wait on land for our inescapable destiny. How could we fight against this sinister magician, who uses her currents like nets to rip them from our loving arms ?

She holds unimaginable treasures in store for them, wealth at hand, distant lands full of adventure and easy girls, but she is only a mermaid, who uses her spells to blind them and turn them into toys of her dark designs. Very few come back from these long journeys, where they often find nothing but disillusionment, illness and ship-wrecks. Death ! Death again and again, by drowning or by sword, by scurvy or pox... The few who come back are as if possessed, and roll their eyes like madmen, swaying on the docks like the drifting souls they have become. Woe to the wives of these lost men, of these ghosts who only dream of leaving without a glance back, as soon as the wind turns and the tide calls them. Damn you, necrophagus, great whore who has put madness in the hearts of my men and snatched them from me ! Or rather, cursed are we poor women, who remain powerless against you. The truth is the lovers of the sea are lost forever... "

The disciple took an inquiring look at his host. Almitra smiled at him :

"It's a refrain that she regularly gives us, one of the few that we still understand. I let her say, it does her good, I think ..."

"She's not necessarily wrong !"

"Maybe... Sailors have always lived this way, and always will. We all accept it. In any case, I hope that the evil that is gnawing at her gives her a little respite when she expresses it that way."

An awkward silence set in, which lasted several minutes. Almitra poured some more wine to give herself some self-control, but didn't dare to ask the questions that were burning her lips. In the end, she knew nothing about the man she had invited to her home, whom anyone would have considered a vagabond of dubious character, to be avoided at all costs. She had acted without thinking, driven by her thirst to know more about Almustafa, and especially about his last moments, and perhaps it was madness...

To her great relief, it was Youssef who tackled the subject first :

"You were very close to the prophet, weren't you ?" he asked.

"Yes, at the time he lived in Orphalese he did not have

many friends. Real friends, I mean. And I think I was one of them."

"He was always apart from men; the acquaintances he had access to made him lonely. He was like an eagle hovering over the banality of human affairs, which didn't even touch him. "

"Were you present when he was arrested? How did it happen? We had little feedback here, where he was portrayed as the worst criminal."

"At the time of the tragedy, his reputation had grown so much that it preceded him everywhere we were going. The people who were coming to listen to him were now moving in ever denser crowds, and we were often greeted by scenes of jubilation in the villages where we were staying.

We soon realized that, beyond his teachings, the healings and miracles which, invented for some of them, forged his legend, he represented a hope of liberation and peace for the regions enslaved and devoured by the war that we sometimes went through.

Some of his parables, repeated and distorted by hundreds of mouths, misunderstood, made him a resistance fighter against the occupying armies, a liberator on a triumphant tour to uplift the people and incite them to take up arms. His fate, from then on, was sealed, and only a spark was missing to stop him.

The day the soldiers took him, I was visiting a member of my family. When I returned to the town where our group had stopped, they had already sentenced him, and they were taking him to the place of his execution. They had accused him of stirring up trouble among the people, spreading ideas of revolt and fomenting attacks against the invader. He was a threat to the ruling power, can you imagine?

On the way to his death by stoning, our eyes met. I had managed to slip into the front row, to speak to him one last time, to support him... He smiled at me, God, he smiled at me... How could he ?"

"Haven't you been troubled ? Did no one recognize you as one of his disciples ?"

The old man was wringing his hands, and his lips were trembling.

"I disowned him," he confessed half-voiced. "I was scared to death, and I denied the Master, just when he needed me the most. Several times, the soldiers questioned me. People pointed their fingers at me, but I hid, I fled, just like all the others. I should have been proud of our ideas, bulged my chest and died beside him that day, but no, I am too much of a coward. I'm unworthy of all the love he gave us. And I am not alone : none of the disciples rose up to defend and protect him. We all hid like rats, waiting for death to look the other way. "Truly, all the teachings of the Beloved had suddenly vanished, and were useless..."

He buried his face in his numb fingers, to hide his emotion and shame.

Then the front door opened in a gale, and a boy burst into the house. He was still very young, probably a dozen or so years old, but his mutinous face, his black hair and his big laughing eyes made him endearing at first glance. His expressions, his lively movements, everything about him sparkled with intelligence.

"This is my only son, Mustapha." said Almitra.

Youssef hastily wiped his wet eyes in his sleeve.

"Well, I think I can guess where this name comes from !" he said with a smile back on his face. He reached out his hand to the child, who shook it vigorously, uncovering a space between his front teeth.

Almitra lowered her eyes and blushed :
"It's true... I couldn't help it !"
She covered her offspring with a look full of pride and tenderness.
"You come from far away, it seems," said Mustapha.
"Indeed I do, my young friend, from the other side of the sea..."
"And are you planning to stay long ?"
"My goodness, I don't know yet, but I might : I'm getting old and tired of running around the world. Would you accept me in your city ?"
The old man took an air of defiance, while the child pretended to think :
"We don't like troublemakers around here," Mustapha said finally, crossing his arms, as if he represented the supreme authority of Orphalese.
"Come on, what danger could an old man like me represent ?" said Youssef with a sweet voice.
Mustapha pouted again for a moment.
"It's alright... But I'll keep an eye on you !" he admitted at last, pointing a threatening finger.
The old man and the child shook hands to seal their agreement, while exchanging a conniving glance.
Almitra stood up and grabbed his son by the arm :
"Stop fooling around and go to bed, I want you to go to school tomorrow, for once !"
The boy obeyed reluctantly, and went to lie down in a nearby room, not without grasping a piece of fruit on the table, which would probably serve as his dinner.
"He's driving me crazy coming home so late. He's got his own agenda. Since his father's missing, I have no authority over him, and he's growing like a weed !"
"I wouldn't worry about him, he seems very smart to me and he'll always be all right."

"I hope so, but at the moment he's using his mischief for bad tricks and nonsense, and I'm afraid of his acquaintances when he spends his days on the streets..."

The worried mother sat down at the table and sighed :

"The thousand preoccupations of daily life sometimes suffocate me, and I feel like I'm brought down to the ground as soon as I try to fly away in spirit. Let's talk about you and Almustafa again, shall we ? How long have you been following him ? How did you meet ?"

As Youssef opened his mouth to tell his story, old Nedjma began to fidget in her armchair and growl more than usual.

"Rise up, women !" she shouted, "And take back the world from the hands of men, who have led it into wandering and chaos !"

Almitra had a pinched smile.

"When she gets to that point in her speech, it is because she kindly lets us know that we are annoying her," she explained.

"Well that's kind of her," sighed Youssef.

"She's got her habits, and it's very late. I have to take care of her and put her to bed. And she wakes up early, the naughty one !"

"It's a heavy burden you're carrying here... How long has it been going on ?"

"I don't know," Almitra thought, "a few years... And it's not over, I'm afraid !"

She put a smile on her face.

"But it's okay, it's what Adel would have wanted. I know that where he is, he's proud of me."

"It's a terrible sacrifice," said the disciple. "You seem to be loved by all, you could start a new life..."

"It seems difficult to me. In any case, who would want an old woman like me, and with a child moreover ? Besides, my son could be useful to me : he could keep Nedjma for a day, while I go for lunch at your place, for example ! You could thus, at your convenience, tell me about your extraordinary adventures, and all that I don't know about the Master's life !"

Disconcerted by the suddenness of this invitation in reverse, Youssef at first didn't know what to answer, then gladly accepted.

That night, it was with an unusually light heart that he climbed the long steep path that took him home in the darkness.

To receive Almitra at home should not have moved Youssef so much. Not only had there been no innuendo in this proposal, but two people of their age, who have been through life several times, do not swoon at the idea of a one-to-one lunch.

However, the old man had lost the habit of this kind of exercise. After years of walking around the world with a satchel slung over his shoulder, begging for his pittance from the good souls he met in exchange of a good story or a bit of work, he no longer knew how to treat a lady.

It didn't take him long to put the little room in order, but it allowed him to make an alarming observation. Supposing one had something to eat to give to the lady, one would still need to have a dish, cutlery, so that she could taste it ! But there was no crockery, except for the nomadic bowl which the disciple had taken everywhere, and which was hardly presentable anyway.

He took his courage in both hands and decided to take the path down to Orphalese. Once in the centre, he questioned many passers-by, looking for a shop that would meet his desires. In the end, in a steep alley not far from the port, he was shown the address of a potter who would be sure to satisfy him. Indeed, the shop was full of objects of all shapes and sizes, which piled up from floor to ceiling and spilled over into the street, where they huddled together on either side of the entrance, along the facade.

There were cups and craters, plates and dishes, vases and cups, amphoras and flasks. All were finely decorated, using various techniques, but always revealed an artist of the highest mastery and inspiration. Scenes from everyday life, fantastical and fabulous animals, mythical heroes' fights, educational allegories, sporting exploits, paraded under the amazed gaze of passers-by, and Youssef in particular. The disciple entered the shop without even thinking about the meagre crockery he wanted to buy, but to meet the brilliant author of so many masterpieces.

To his great surprise, he discovered a young woman sitting behind her wheel, whose slender hands were plunged into the grey, dripping clay. The woman greeted her visitor with a sober nod, without saying a word. She stubbornly kept her eyes raised to the sky, as if in a deep inspiration, and it took Youssef several minutes to realize that they were abnormally clear. The modeller was blind !

She agreed with a smile when the disciple asked her if he could stay for a while to watch her work. Fascinated by the precision of the artist's gestures, Youssef sat down on the bare earth floor, soothed by the regular beat of the pedal that operated the wheel. The slender fingers were unhesitatingly sinking into the clay, which suddenly opened into a corolla, or climbed up in a phantasmagorical colonnade, as if by magic.

The ceramist was not beautiful in the strict sense of the word, but she was so graceful that the traveller could not take his eyes off her. The proximity of a firing kiln made the heat in the workshop stifling, and forced her to work in very light clothing. She wrapped the wheel between her bare legs, so that one would have said that her creations were like children that literally came from her womb, as a maternal magician with extraordinary powers.

In front of the obvious symbolism of this scene, and

the incredible beauty of the pieces that came out of the shapeless matter in front of him, Youssef thought he heard the Prophet whisper a teaching in his ear :

"The artist is a translator of worlds. His heightened sensitivity gives him access to dimensions that the common man cannot even imagine. He brings back sensations, images, sounds, which he tries to retranscribe as best he can through his art, so that his fellow mortals can benefit from them.

This is where the work and the practice of the tool take place. Whether it is through clay, a brush or a flute, the artist is confronted with the resistance of matter, its heaviness, its slowness. He has at his disposal instruments that he has to tame in order to restore his emotion in a way that is closest to the original spark that he felt in his soul. It is in this passage from inspiration to work that the artist's life is at stake. It is his mastery of the medium and the gesture that will allow him, little by little, year after year, to reduce the difference between the result of his work and his first intuitive vision.

A channel is then created between his mind and his hand, which he will spend his whole existence purifying, in order to eliminate as much as possible the distorting filter of the thoughts.

The master is the one whose hand is directly controlled by vision, by lightning. In his creative phase, he then truly enters a state of trance and his senses are cut off from the outside world. He will stop, exhausted but fulfilled, only when the work stands before him, perfect in its completion, brought by him out of nothingness, as he had dreamed it.

One will then call "genius" a master endowed by nature with a greater memory, or greater ease of learning, and who has thus reduced to a minimum the period of domestication of the instrument by his hand, of purification of his creative channel. The time thus gained allows him to go faster and further towards the perfection of his creation. He rises one degree above men, on the infinite scale that leads to divinity. For God is the first of the artists, whose work is in perpetual elaboration..."

The squealing of a piece of furniture being moved into the adjacent room took the old man out of his meditation. Pushed by curiosity, and without making a sound, he put his head behind the curtain that separated the two parts of the shop.

There he discovered a poor deformed being, crawling on the floor because of atrophied limbs. His hands too were affected by the evil, and they seemed to be permanently tight, twisted and blocked at an angle that made them unusable.

His face, however, was most comely, and the resemblance to the modeller was astonishing : twins, no doubt. The cripple greeted his visitor with a dazzling smile and went back to his work :

This part of the workshop was indeed his domain. Everything had been placed at his level, and an unimaginable palette of colors was spread out there.

"Is there anything I can do for you ?" asked the young man.

"Well, I'm simply stunned by the quality of your productions," replied Youssef. "Can I watch you work ?"

"Of course, clients often do, although many of them come especially to admire my sister, Alhena. They think she doesn't see them, but she is sensitive to many other things, much more subtle, and she knows everything that's going on ! Besides, something tells me she doesn't mind, although her shyness makes her stingy with words."

"It's true that she's charming, but my advanced age

obliges me too to be interested in more subtle things ! These are real works of art that come out of your studio, and I could contemplate them for hours..."

"We've gained notoriety, indeed, and objects stamped 'Alhena and Munir' are selling better and better, and further and further ! Many ships and caravans transport our collections to the far sides of the world, and we sometimes get very exotic orders."

"I'm happy for you, it's only fair."

Munir grabbed a vase that Alhena had finished a few hours earlier, and cleverly wedged it against him. Then he plunged a blowtorch into a coloured cup, and began to blow on the surface of the virgin earth, which had turned white as it dried. In a few minutes a ship appeared, sails inflated, ready to set sail for legendary shores.

To see this pair of twins working together on the same creations, making the most of each other's talents while ignoring the handicaps that nature had imposed on them, was a real life lesson for the disciple. More than that, it was a symbolic vision of the march of the universe as Almustafa had tried to explain it to him, with concepts that he had found difficult to grasp :

"Two great forces presided over the creation of the world, in the primal explosion that transformed the uncreated into the created, darkness into light, nothingness into matter. They can be called "Will" and "Desire" , or "Movement" and "Attraction" , or simply "Male" and "Female" .

These two forces, stemming from the Divine Consciousness, are both irreconcilable and inseparable, and it is the enormous tensions between them, born of the will and desire for creation of the Source of Being, that caused the initial explosion.

The first represents the male component of the universe,

the movement, the will, the clear, the clear, the warm, the active, the fire. It provokes change, conquest, adventure, decision.

The second, the female component, represents immobility, desire, darkness, cold, passive, water. It provokes waiting, nesting, maturation, reflection.

We see how complementary and necessary they are to life in all its forms, and how their principles can be applied to everything that exists in Creation."

Seeing Munir blowing his colours, Youssef thought that creating was perhaps just that, an act both simple and essential : to inject beauty into chaos. Another sentence of the Master imposed itself on his mind :

"Matter is not only inseparable from consciousness, but they are in fact two forms of the same original substance. During the initial explosion, many droplets of the Divine Consciousness were blown into Creation, and intimately mixed with matter, down to the smallest particles of which it is composed. In fact, matter is consciousness made visible. Thus, there is not a degree of complexity in life for which one could define the beginning of consciousness (the plant kingdom ? the animal kingdom ? humankind ? and why not the mineral ?). Any material entity can be subdivided into smaller entities, which have their own levels of consciousness. And this, whether we go to the infinitely small or the infinitely vast ..."

It was only much later, at last satiated with beauty and metaphysics, that the disciple decided to leave, carrying a delicate dinner service under his arm. Would his calamus succeed in properly writing down such intangible teachings ?

As soon as Youssef came back from the twin artists' shop, he put his purchases on his mattress and rushed to his work table to compose on paper the most sublime sentences imaginable. What Alhena and Munir were accomplishing with clay, he wanted to achieve with his ink. But as his calamus floated in the air above the white sheet of paper, the old man was suddenly crushed by the extent of his ignorance. How does one find a worthy sentence ? How do you mark the memory of men ? How do you assemble letters so that they arouse images, and even emotions ? How can one transmit one's knowledge without being boring ?

Perhaps, by way of introduction, we should start his story of the Prophet with Almustafa's teaching on the ceremony of drawing lines in consciousness on paper, that is, by loading each line with a meaning, and thus an action on the world. He said that there is a sorcery that surrounds words, and that drawing characters with meaning is a sacred act.

Youssef felt even more dizzy. He saw the Master again, sitting on the ground among the disciples, drawing a strange symbol in the sand before speaking :

"There is a mysterious link, so to speak magical, so powerful and inexplicable, which unites the thought, the spoken and the written word. Thought, speech and writing must be considered as three parallel worlds, three keys that are activated successively, three stages that a concept must go through imperatively to pass from the subtle to the material, from the uncreated to the created, from the non-existent to the existing.

For a project, or a creation, to take shape and materialize, it must leave the mental sphere in which it was conceived. But before reaching the material sphere, in which it will be visible to the eyes of all, it must most often pass through the verbal sphere, which puts the idea into form, and begins to communicate it around the creator. The word can therefore be considered as the first step in the materialization of a concept. The verb is the beginning of creation, the primordial tool for transforming matter into the receptacle of the idea.

Thus, the Creator pronounced the name of everything in the cold darkness of the origins, and this simple chant engendered the universe. And yourselves, hear well, were one of His dreams, then a whisper in His mouth, before appearing in this world.

How many artists struggle to see their ideas materialize because they remain silent ? If they talked about their work, about their projects in gestation around them, they would set in motion incalculable forces that would favour the advent of creation by preparing the world for its coming existence !"

A few days later, Youssef began his investigation to discover what remained of the passage of the Prophet in the memory of the inhabitants of Orphalese. He decided to go to the temple, because that was where it all began.

The entrance to the sanctuary opened onto a vast inner courtyard, surrounded by grey stone columns. The floor was entirely covered with heavy, colourful brocade carpets on which one walked barefoot. The faithful liked to meet there, before or after the service, and it had become a sort of forum where the most diverse subjects were discussed, where news was exchanged, and where the most daring could launch public controversies.

That morning, when the old disciple entered, the forum was empty, and only a group of young novices, recognizable by their long white tunic and shaved heads, animated the space.

It was customary for the aspirants to the priesthood, in between lessons given by an elder, to sharpen their rhetoric and their minds among themselves, addressing controversial points of the law. On a thorny subject, the group would split into two, each of them making their arguments with varying degrees of ardour and fervour, until the noise of their quarrel disturbed one of their masters sufficiently to make him come and decide for himself on a sentence that could not be appealed. The faithful who passed by were allowed to take part in the debates, and that is why no one paid any attention to Youssef when he sat down with the young people to listen to what they were saying.

After several minutes of fruitless arguments, he took the floor :

"How do you think Almustafa would have approached this problem ?" he asked.

He wanted to know if the Master's words were still alive among the younger generations, especially those who were destined for religion. The reaction he provoked was not the expected one, and there was a great disapproving silence.

"You are undoubtedly one of those who called him a Prophet !" said the most virulent one, probably the leader of the band, in a contemptuous tone. And they stared at him from head to toe, frowning.

"Certainly, and I make no secret of it," replied Youssef, thinking that the sadness of his shaggy clothes and his shaggy hair had become, with time and travel, the rallying signs of the followers of Almustafa.

"You don't carry it in your heart, one would say," replied the old man, who had become the focus of all eyes.

"He wasn't a prophet, but a preacher !" said another. "A desert magician, an illusionist !"

"It's men like him who blur the divine message, leading simple souls down the wrong path !" said a third.

Youssef was flabbergasted by such vehemence, and did not see what in Almustafa's message could provoke it.

"Much has been said about him, so much so that he became a legend," said the first novice. "Ever since he came to Orphalese, everyone has been infatuated with him. He has turned people away from the true faith, and our temples are empty. Our best preachers are unable to convince them as he, it seems, could. He was certainly a good talker, and he must not have lacked charisma. But his sweet words, full of love and good feelings, he put them at his service. There was no room in his heart for anyone but himself. He was a proud, ambitious man who relished the adoration of the crowds. I tell you the truth, he was not in the service of God, but of his own glory !"

"You say his words were love, what's wrong with that ?"

"His words were not in accord with his deeds. You followed him, you say ? Then what do you think of his so-called miracles ? He healed the sick by laying his hands on the wounds, didn't he ? It's even said that he brought dead people back to life !"

"Certainly," said Youssef, "I've witnessed many of these extraordinary healings... Isn't that proof of his enlightenment ? Of his blessing by the Creator to show us the powers we should all have ?"

"Don't you understand that it was all a trick ? Skillfully staged to increase her power over the crowd ? He knew that the crowd, hungry for heroes, would immediately amplify his words and deeds to forge his reputation !"

Another boy took over :

"By the way, who was he before he was suddenly 'enlightened' ? Didn't he often hang out in the taverns with the dregs of the rabble ? Didn't he hang out with prostitutes ? How can you believe that virtue suddenly fell on his shoulders, except by an odious calculation allowing him an easy life by swindling gullible spirits ?"

Youssef, overwhelmed by so many preconceived ideas and slanders, did not at first know how to respond.

"It is because he knew us so well," he tried, "in every aspect of our lives, that he found the images that spoke directly to our hearts, and that even the illiterate, the uneducated poor, understood his message... His teachings were free from all existing philosophies ; he went beyond them, making them obsolete by their modernity ; he opened the doors to universal understanding !"

At these words, the young men burst out laughing, giving each other complicit burps.

"You're old," they concluded, "and we know we can't change your mind. We young people are more sensible. We would never take credit for the words of a self-centered pathological liar..."

They rose up quickly, for their teacher had entered the courtyard, and disappeared after him, mocking the disciple. Youssef sat alone in the sun in the middle of the forum and put his hand through his thick beard, lost in his thoughts.

"WELL, my son," said someone behind his back, "you look very concerned. Would a friendly voice make you feel better ?"

Youssef turned around and discovered an old man, twisted by the weight of years, who had difficulty supporting himself with a cane. He probably was over eighty years old.

"I am the oldest priest in Orphalese," said the man. "I'm usually called 'the Dean', or 'the Venerable'. Some even say 'the Wise One', but nothing is less certain... However, if you need to unburden your soul, perhaps I can be of service ?"

He had the weary smile of those who have seen so much that they do not expect much.

"I spoke with a group of novices," said Youssef.

The priest laughed heartily :

"They must still have a lot to learn, if they left you in this state !"

"We don't have the same opinion of Almustafa."

"Ah ! That one again."

The wrinkled face closed.

"You knew him, I believe ?" asked the venerable one after a moment of reflection.

"I followed him for a long time, until the end." Youssef replied.

The old man nodded his head, and squinted his eyes

so that there was no sign of envy.

"Almustafa made me understand something terrible," he sighed. "God isn't here anymore..."

Youssef stared at him, surprised.

"Every day, the faithful become fewer and fewer," the priest said. "Our celebrations have become nothing but sinister farces. Soon, only bigots and fanatics will be left to visit our temples again. I tell you the truth, God is no longer here : He has taken to the streets. Your prophet understood this before all of us. He loved mankind, and desired mankind to love itself. That is why he went out to meet people and spoke to them about God in the market place. We, the guardians of the law, are cut off from the realities of this world, and God has abandoned us."

The disciple kept silent, for he had not imagined such an earthquake. The hoarse voice continued his monologue, as if it were his own :

"When Almustafa arrived in this isolated city, he was just a young man with a thirst for the absolute. When he left, he was a mature man who had found such intense faith that he was ready to sow the world with his visions. And he had accomplished this wonder in only twelve short years ! I, too, was just over twenty years old when I came to take up my ministry at Orphalese. But contemplate my distress, O brother ! Sixty years later, I am just beginning to understand a few snippets of His Word ! Truly, I now know that He was a great Prophet."

A deep silence marked this confession. Then the voice resumed, as if tinged with a vague smile, seeking to revive images almost erased :

"I sometimes heard him talking in the square, or outside the taverns, for he mingled with the crowd in his simplest pleasures. I should have finally known what he was going to say, and yet he surprised me every time. I know it now, he wouldn't learn anything by heart, he would make it up as he went along, depending on the context and the questions he was asked. He picked the words out of the air around him, like cherry blossoms that nature itself would have put at his disposal to please him. Then he would blow these words gently over his subdued listeners, and I could see their eyes widening in understanding, and their lips smiling with appeasement. Hear me well, brother : I saw these simple souls enlightened before my eyes, and touched by a grace, a deep knowledge, such as I have never been able to give birth to in my most assiduous flocks !"

*

* *

Youssef was long gone, and the sky was already beginning to turn to gold when the Venerable retired to the small study room which he loved so much, the one next to his room and which, like most of the rooms of the temple, was devoid of all comforts. The empty walls, whitewashed with lime, reflected the sun that entered through many openings, materializing the divine spirit that was supposed to inspire the scribes who spent their days copying the Holy Word. The luminosity of the place, the soft carpets, the surrounding silence, everything led to sacredness and introspection.

He unlocked a chest to which only he had the key and took out a large roll of parchment, which seemed to fall to dust with the slightest breath, so worn was it by the generations who had handled it. The old man carried the scroll to a table, which was not easy for him, for it was heavy and bulky, and then unrolled it for a moment until it fell on a passage which he found interesting.

He quickly absorbed himself in his reading, swinging imperceptibly back and forth, his twisted finger slowly following the lines as his dry lips moved silently, chanting the words of God.

Of course, after so many years, his eyes were damaged from repeating this exercise day after day, and he guessed the words more than he read them. He'd known them in his heart for so long...

Each day he took this precious time to meditate on the day that had passed, to take counsel of God and himself, to become more immersed in The Law, of which he was the heir and the bearer. The Law ! Imperative commandments and sublime songs, the history of humanity, the most sacred knowledge of the workings of the universe, dictated by God to his prophets, written by God himself, perhaps, centuries ago ! Nothing could be added to it, nothing could be taken away from it without offending the Creator and plunging the world into chaos. The balance of civilization rested on the respect of the Law, and nothing and no one could question it. In this, Almustafa had committed an unforgivable crime, which was punishable by death.

It was at this point that the novice he had called respectfully entered the room with his hands folded in front of him as a sign of humility. One would not have thought, on seeing him, that he had been one of Youssef's most ferocious mockers during the morning, only a few hours before.

"A stranger has arrived in the city," said the venerable without preamble.

"You mean the disciple of Almustafa ?"

"Yes, the heretic, that's right... I think he is dangerous. I've heard of him, he was one of his closest followers. I am convinced he came to stir up trouble."

"What can we do, your holiness ?"

"Keep an eye on the man, and notify the aedile Zain. Tell him a foreign preacher has just arrived in the city, who may be disrupting law and order. We are the people's bond, and it is our duty to preserve civil peace."

THE next day at noon, at the appointed hour, Almitra arrived at the outskirts of the shepherd's house. She did not have to knock on the door, because it opened by itself. Youssef, both anxious and impatient, went out regularly to watch the way.

The weather was surprisingly calm for these heights, and the clear sky hinted at a milder than usual afternoon.

"You are definitely living at the end of the world," said the lady as she tried to catch her breath.

"It's true that at my age, this road is a test," Youssef replied as he let her in. "But I expect that this exercise repeated from time to time will keep me in good shape ! It also has the advantage of keeping the unwelcome away, which is not negligible !"

"You don't count me among those, I hope ?" she smiled.

"On the contrary, Madam : to receive the queen of the market of Orphalese is the greatest of honours," said the disciple, and curtseyed.

They sat down on either side of the little writing table that stood there, which had been transformed into a banquet table for the occasion, but which, once covered with the two plates and two cups of earth recently acquired, left no room for the dishes !

The noble guest complimented Youssef on the beauty of his tableware, and the cleanliness of his modest interior, while the old man uncorked a jug of thick, fragrant red wine and filled the cups with it.

"I opened my heart to you the other night and told you a part of my life," he said, resting the jug at the foot of the table. "And now it's your turn : Tell me about yourself and the Beloved. How did your friendship come about ?"

"Like you, I met Almustafa the day he arrived, and first, I think, I detected in this young man a flame, a thirst for truth and absoluteness that never wavered afterwards. I had a strange power then, which had brought me into the temple, and it was on his steps that I met him, freshly landed, from his native island."

"*Strange power*, you say ? You have piqued my curiosity ! What was it all about ? And have you lost that power ?"

"I was, and to a lesser extent still am, endowed with clairvoyance : I sense and see things that are beyond the reach of ordinary mortals. I hear the voices of the dead, I know the story of an object I hold in my hand, I anticipate the arrival of an illness long before the first symptoms appear... All these gifts made me a special member of the Orphalesian society. Even the priests of the temple had reserved a room in the sanctuary for me so that the people could come and consult me."

"Unbelievable ! You were some kind of prophetess yourself, then ! No wonder you got along with the Master... But I'm surprised that the priests welcomed you into their midst like this. They could have condemned you for witchcraft !"

"I was just coming out of childhood, and it wasn't easy at first. But I had cured several of them, who came to see me in secret, and I had announced to them many events that later proved to be true. Since my good intentions were never taken for granted, that I was not questioning the

Law, they concluded that it was God who was working through me, and they considered me as one of their own. Over the years, I became the seer in the temple, the one who was consulted to explain the invisible mysteries of the world... the one who gave the divine answers to the existential anguish of the inhabitants of Orphalese."

"It's fascinating ! I didn't know anything about your past. Almustafa had never mentioned it. Was it your gift that helped you see in him what he would become ?"

"Maybe, I don't know. I immediately felt a special affinity, very strong, between our two souls. Like two old acquaintances meeting again after a long separation. During the twelve years that followed, we maintained a privileged friendship, where we did not hide anything from each other about our respective questions and developments. I can say that I was one of her rare friends, because her distant attitude was misunderstood by the people here. As he preferred solitude, as he spent his time far from the city, on the heights and in the forest, he was taken for a misanthrope, a proud or a marginalist..."

"It's a feeling I know well !"

"It wasn't until he finally left that everyone realized how important his place was in the community, and his last words to the locals, just before he got on the boat that took him away from us, were the most beautiful words he ever said to us."

"Your life then was not at all like the one you lead today... You're no longer part of the temple, what happened ?"

"Almustafa's departure was more traumatic than I thought. Before he left, he taught us about love, marriage, children, all the things that make up a woman's life and that I had never really paid attention to, because I had devoted myself entirely to my mission. As I listened to him speak, and on the verge of losing him probably forever, I suddenly missed him, and I began to feel a great emptiness inside me.

The years that followed seemed long and tasteless. I no longer knew how to lead my life, I felt useless and lost. The priests' view of the world and of God seemed limited, narrow and sclerotic to me, since I had seen the light in the teachings of the Master. The days in the temple no longer brought me any joy, but I dared not leave my service.

However, one day I met Adel there. He had come to pray for his father, who had disappeared at sea. We fell in love with each other and I left everything to go and live with him. Soon, as I thought my time was up, we were blessed with a son, whom you know."

Youssef served some wine to his host :

"And your clairvoyance, what has become of it ?"

"I hardly use it anymore. Sometimes people come to me at home for advice, and I do some services, but I don't trade them."

Almitra had finished her story, and she took a few sips to moisten her lips, dry from talking so much.

"I have given myself up more than I thought," she said to the disciple, "but it's up to you now. Answer my curiosity, which has remained unsatisfied since Nedjma interrupted us : How did you meet the Master ?"

THE traveller, in turn, emptied his cup before beginning his story :

"The crowd of people following him was already large when Almustafa stopped in the town of Pyrimar, where I was living at the time. Everywhere, his reputation preceded him, and his arrival made a great noise.

I was a schoolmaster, a science lover and an astronomy enthusiast. I made it a point of honour to live far from any religious consideration, and these stories of the so-called prophet did not concern me. I had developed, I must say, a rather cynical atheism, and considered priests as liars, abusing their power over poor people.

However, after a few days, the insistent rumours of repeated miracles, of incredible healings, reached me. Everywhere in the streets, people spoke of him, and some, with a smile on their lips, said they were converted, called him the Beloved, and repeated his words which, according to them, had touched their hearts.

So much so that I too decided to join the group of curious people who gravitated around the square where Almustafa gave his teachings. I thought I was smarter than the little people, and I felt ready to denounce a charlatan, and dismantle his illusions in public ! Just think : it was even said that he could raise the dead !

The crowd was so great, and the assembly so compact, that I could not get near Almustafa. I couldn't see or hear him, and I was very angry. I had a rather bad temper at that time, I must admit. So I decided to climb a tree and jump on a high terrace. Thus, from terrace to balcony, from roof to roof, I was able to get as close as possible to the Master, just above the colonnades under which he had settled.

I could hear his deep and melodious voice, almost singing, but I could only understand every other word, I was still too far away. I could see the faces of the listeners, alternately concentrated or laughing, nodding at the leader, elbowing each other when an anecdote had hit the spot. At one point I leaned so far over the void that the beam on which I was broke under my weight; I fell heavily in the middle of the audience, provoking general hilarity.

"Here is an angel fallen from heaven," said the speaker with a smile. "Is what I am saying so astounding ?"

"Some say it is, indeed," I replied as I got up, and tried to regain some composure. "It seems that you speak of God as no one else does, and that you captivate your audiences with wonderful tales. But I confess that I have little taste for the faribbles of religious and preachers. You see, I'm a rational, science-loving man, and their wonderful stories have never withstood a well-established demonstration based on irrefutable proof !"

A disapproving murmur ran through the spectators, who were obviously sympathetic to his cause.

"I say that science is another form of religion," he replied, "which has its sclerotic priests and its beliefs, its lies and its blinkers."

"I can easily imagine what you say to those who follow you, for I have heard a lot of nonsense coming out of 'holy mouths' revered by simple minds. It is easy to describe the paradisiacal shores of the afterlife, or the ocean of darkness of the universe's beginnings, for no one has been able to explore these intangible realms."

"Truly, I tell you : the man of science relies only on what he can observe, or infer by reason from what he can observe. In so doing he trusts in what his senses bring back to him in visible forms, and his scaffolding of ever-bolder theories rests only on sand, for what he knows is only a tiny portion of what is."

"Too easy !" I said scornfully.

"Ask a scientist why his heart beats, and he'll tell you about nerve impulses, ebb and flow, how much blood to purify... He'll explain in detail how it all works. The best surgeon could open the organ and repair it. But no one will tell you what it's all for ! What is the primary cause of this debauchery of intelligence and mechanisms, which beats perfectly millions of times during your lifetime without you needing to worry about it ? Who is the Designer, and what is His purpose ?"

I didn't want to continue making a fool of myself in public, and I had an idea :

"Would you like to come to my house for dinner to-night ? We could confront our views more quietly ?"

"I'd like that, but would you agree to invite the city beggars, who haven't had a decent meal in years, to your house ? Look at me. Don't I have the makings of a beggar myself ? My clothes are coloured by the dust of the roads, pierced by thorns, discoloured by the winds... Why should you invite me, and not my comrades in misfortune ? You want us to debate, you thirst for truth and certainty, but wouldn't the greatest lesson come from those you consider least ?"

I took him at his word, and so it was done ! When evening came, I left my door open, and many of the inhabitants who had attended the invitation came forward, as well as admirers of Almustafa who followed him on the roads. My house was very small, so few people could get in, and anyway, I could not feed many people. Howe-ver, I distributed what I had to all the poor bums who had crowded around my house, too happy with the chance that was offered to them. As a host, I had the chance to spend the evening by the side of Almustafa. I found him simple, accessible. He was a pleasant, witty guest, who could be a lot of fun. For a so-called holy man, he ate and drank wine like anyone else, and didn't seem to bend to any particular life discipline. Had it not been for his notoriety, he might have been a commonplace guest, passing unnoticed in the midst of laughs and conversations.

However, towards the end of the meal, he was asked questions and prayed to speak again. He told us stories that fascinated us as he drew inspiration from our daily lives. He always succeeded in transforming these innocuous fables into deep visions that made us tremble at our bases, so much so that they questioned our most fundamental beliefs, which had always seemed obvious to us.

We listened to him all night long, without tiredness, as if wrapped in a spell. Little by little, I understood how empty my life was, and I glimpsed an unknown world, much larger than anything I had imagined. When in the morning he took his leave, thanking me for my welcome, I felt that I could no longer do without the living source of his teachings.

A few weeks later, the Prophet set out again and left Pyrimar, and I decided to take to the road with his com-panions. Overnight, I gave up everything : my job, my house, my past. My friends called me crazy, and tried to hold me back, but the life they represented now seemed vain and useless to me. One might have thought that I had been manipulated, even bewitched, to change my life so brutally, on a whim. And maybe I was, but I've never regretted it since. Most of the people who listened to him did not radically change course, I rather think that my field had been ploughed before, and was ready to receive the ideas that the Master was trying to sow there.

We lived like that for a few years, going from town to town, being lodged by relatives of one or the other, often sleeping in the open air, under the stars. The troop of travelling companions kept growing. He chose some of us, whom he called disciples, with whom he spent more time to give them privileged explanations. How did he select them, and why was I one of them ? I will never know... Anyway, I was lucky enough to spend the most beautiful moments of my life in his company.

It was clear to all of us that he knew his presence among us was short-lived, and he wanted to pass on to us what he had learned from his enlightenment so that we could continue his work after him. We obviously refused to contemplate such a cataclysm at the time, for he was the air and water we needed for our lives, and it was unthinkable that we could survive without him.

Yet that is what happened shortly afterwards, as you know. After the tragedy, I did what Almustafa expected us to do. I walked, I criss-crossed the seaside in all directions, going further and further, exploring plains and mountains to meet peoples whose existence I had not known until then.

"These are extraordinary adventures," said Almitra. "It is absolutely necessary to write all this down, so that future generations will remember it ! How were you welcomed in those faraway lands ?"

"Quite well, to tell the truth. I felt the presence of the Master when I was in difficulty, and the doors opened naturally when I needed them. What I told of his life, and what I had understood from his teachings, was so universal, so beautiful when I managed to render its poetry, that I was encouraged to stay and settle in the villages I passed through."

"And you were never tempted ?"

"Oh yes, many times ! And I've often given in, I admit... I sometimes stayed for several years in communities where I felt at home. But always, one day or another, a strange force pushed me to go back on the road, even if reluctantly. There are so many souls to meet in the world, so many encounters to make..."

There was melancholy in the old man's voice, and a hint of moisture in his eyes. Was it the magnitude of the task at hand, so immense that he had only scratched the surface, or was it the unspeakable memory of joys gone forever ? Almitra modestly looked away to the opening above the table that let the daylight into the hovel. In the distance, the sound of the surf and seagulls seemed unreal.

"And now you are with us," said the lady of Orphalese with a beautiful smile.

"Yes, I think this is the end of the road," replied the disciple. "I have pain everywhere, and I am too old to continue. I want to devote what energy and memory I have left to write down the words of Almustafa."

"It's a wise decision, and a work of the utmost importance ! I will help you as much as I can."

Thus, grasping their clay cups, they toasted to their budding collaboration, united by the memory of the Beloved Prophet.

IN the days following Almitra's visit, Youssef decided to get down to serious work. He didn't have to go back down to the city for a long time, and he began to explore the surrounding hills and forests, getting further and further away for days on end. He knew that this was the way Almustafa had lived, just a few decades ago, and he wanted to walk in his footsteps, soaking up the same landscapes, meditating under the same trees, secretly hoping that the same enlightenment would come to seize him one day, by surprise.

During one of these long solitary walks, the disciple saw in the distance, in a recess of the cliff, several columns of black smoke rising up in the azure. Alarmed, he immediately diverted himself, in order to bring some help if necessary. After half an hour's walk along a small path on the edge of the void, he came to the top of an imposing conch, at the bottom of which stretched a vast sandy beach from which the fires came.

Youssef saw a man, alone, who seemed to be carrying various debris scattered along the seashore, to assemble them into heaps. It was obvious that he then set them on fire when the pile had reached a sufficient size. There was thus a whole series of mounds more or less aligned at regular intervals, some still burning, others already almost extinguished.

Devoured by curiosity, the disciple wanted to know

what was going on there, and set out to join the mysterious arsonist. He almost broke his neck several times as he descended the steep wall, but finally arrived on the sand.

"Hello !" He shouted to the stranger as he walked in his direction.

The man took a look at him, but didn't stop in his effort. As he approached, Youssef was able to detail him better. Small and slightly stooped, he was already old, though younger than the disciple. His skin was parchment, cooked and wrinkled by the sun and salt. The way he walked revealed the sailor, and the characteristic shape of his hands suggested that he was a fisherman. An old lover of the sea, as Nedjma would have said.

"What happened here ?" Youssef asked. "What are you burning ?"

"Wrecks," answered the chiselled man laconically. "Dismembered ships, pieces of hulls, spars, yards, masts, sterns, bows, sails, ropes... All that was once a proud vessel, carrying men around the world, and now the sea throws back to this coast."

"What happened to them ?"

"War, of course," said the other one darkly. "Since it began, dead ships have been coming here. To the rhythm of successive naval battles, no doubt brought by the currents... It never stops : when I finish cleaning in the evening, everything has to be redone the next morning ! The men are crazy..."

Youssef embraced the beach with a glance, and took the measure of the task that the sailor had set himself with the considerable number of burning mounds.

"But why waste your days in this futile work ?" he asked. "Why not just leave the wood to rot in its place ?"

The other shook his head negatively.

"Nature is beautiful here, the wild and untamed coast,

untouched by the sacking of men. I don't want it to be sullied by our madness. One day the war will end, and that will be the end of my efforts. In the meantime, I'm trying to contain the damage."

Looking closer, Youssef saw that the scum was soiled with a dark, slimy substance, and deposited it on the shore. This thick liquid was floating between two waters, agglutinating in patches, and trapping fish and birds whose sticky bodies, still moving sometimes, multiplied in the surf before running aground.

"Naphtha oil," explained the fisherman. "A new monstrosity of our kind. An accursed substance extracted from the putrid depths of the earth, and until now used only for caulking the hulls of ships. Today, it is a new weapon of war, transported in large quantities from one end of the world to the other, which can be used to set fire to a city or a squadron from a distance. The only way to get rid of it is to burn it, and that's no easy task, believe me !

As for trying to save the contaminated animals, don't even think about it, it's impossible ! That's why I come back here every day, praying that the night hasn't given me more than my daily dose of toil..."

The fisherman probably did not often have the opportunity to vent his bile with such an attentive interlocutor, and words seemed to come more easily to him, revealing a philosopher behind a gruff facade.

"In his blind stubbornness to try to destroy his brother - something which, after all, he could be left free to do - man also makes all forms of life around him disappear, which is unforgivable. Thus, since the beginning of the war, the greatest battles have been fought at sea. It seems that the destiny of the world will be played out on the waves, and it is to who, at each engagement, will line up the most ships. The daily losses are colossal, and the shipyards are multiplying. I have been told that some areas, once covered with deep and game-rich forests, are now arid deserts. All the trees have been turned into ships and then, quite quickly, into wrecks and graves for the poor buggers who had the misfortune to serve on board.

Since we don't see the end of the battles coming, it's likely that within a few years all the shores of the sea will be turned into peeled hills, around an ocean of bones rotting in black, stinking waters."

Youssef shivered when he heard the description of these doomed days, and said nothing. He let the man return to his mission, but could not take his eyes off the long line of blazes that made the creek look like hell.

B Y the end of the day, the weather had changed abruptly, and an icy wind began to blow from the sea. In a few moments the horizon had turned grey, and soon there was an outpouring of dark volutes which galloped towards the continent like a herd of panic-stricken horses with foaming nostrils, fleeing from an obscure menace.

Unimpressed, little Mustapha climbed the path on the edge of the cliff that led to the disciple's hut, a huge bundle on his shoulder. Arriving in front of the door, he casually knocked with his foot on the wooden post, already very agitated by the gusts of wind.

"Hello, old man, are you there ?"

Faced with the lack of reaction from the tenant of the house, the child repeated his blows and calls several times.

"Are you there, old Youssef, or has the approaching storm left you trembling under the table ?"

"Who dares to speak to me in that tone ?" the disciple replied at last, opening his door. He frowned with a terrible eyebrow, which simulated a terrible anger. "Will I have to go to a desert island to work in peace ? Is it you, brat, who bawls me out like that ? I'm no longer surprised that I don't understand anything you're saying : are the words you use too big for your young mouth, or is it your mother's milk, which you haven't finished swallowing, that prevents you from articulating properly ?"

Mustapha smiled with all his teeth. He liked the grumpy

old man, and the conversation had taken a pleasing turn :

"Make it clear I'm not here for my own pleasure," said the boy, "but to obey my mother, who is eating her heart out over you."

"Really ? And why is that ?"

"I told you there's a storm coming, and they're often terrible around here. She gave me some sheets and towels to plug up your window and the holes in your door. It's going to be a very long night !"

"You'll thank Almitra for me, but I'm not even sure this shanty will stand up to the first wind !"

"Don't worry, the walls are thick. This shanty, as you say, is surely older than you, if that's possible, and has withstood many other challenges !"

The two of them soon had every crack in the house sealed. Little Mustapha then hastened to leave his host to go swimming in the creek one last time before the storm arrived, despite the warnings of his elder. Youssef soon saw him go down from rock to rock until he reached the pebble beach. Without the slightest hesitation, the boy sank into the foam, which was probably very cold.

As he watched in the distance Mustapha swimming towards the open sea, tossed like a straw by the swell which, although already very impressive, was still growing, a word of the Prophet came back to his mind, which he swore to write down as soon as he had the opportunity :

"The ages of the world are like the seasons," he said. "While some are gentle and easy to live with, others are sharp as frost or biting as flame, and bruise those who pass through them. Most souls born in these times of suffering complain and blame the Creator with their curse.Some, however, take great pleasure in braving the dangers and upheavals of these chaotic times, and plunge into them with delight, for the sake of play and excitement."

Part II

Praxilas

THE day after the storm, when the morning was still young, the inhabitants of Orphalese who were going out on their doorstep became aware that their little paradise, which had been away from the world for so long, had just been struck to the heart. The age and its torments, accompanied by its procession of fear, violence and suffering, had finally caught up with them, although they thought they had definitively outrun it.

Indeed, at the first light of dawn, a gigantic warship, as dark as night, had overtaken the breakers protecting the harbour cove, and had cast its shadow over the city. Whose side was it on ? No one here would have been able to tell, despite the insignia and coats of arms that marked the stern and flags.The invasions had been going on for many years, but the people of Orphalese, who had been spared so far, held to the strictest neutrality, and took little interest in the echoes of the battles, defeats or victories, which came from time to time. The invasions had been going on for many years, but the people of Orphalese, who had been spared so far, held to the strictest neutrality, and took little interest in the echoes of the battles, defeats or victories, which came from time to time, several months delayed. Perhaps they were hoping, in their candor, that by modestly turning their eyes away from the horrors of war, these would remain far away forever, and would not slaughter any of their children ?

But the sprawling hydra had a boundless appetite and had been playing with the city all this time : now it suddenly appeared in his bosom, without anyone seeing it coming, or being able to do anything about it.

The dark shape, all armored with metal plates and stingers, was advancing slowly, silently, in the middle of the harbor. No one could see a living soul on board, so it looked like a wounded whale that had come to take refuge from the chaos of the night in a calmer bay.

Very quickly the men had massed on the wharves before the intruder came ashore. Sailors and fishermen, merchants and longshoremen, farmers and officials, pressed shoulder to shoulder, perhaps a little for bravado, but probably also to comfort each other in the face of the dark threat that could put their families in danger. Their trained eyes immediately saw on the monster's flanks the traces of its battle against the elements, and indeed its mutilated hull and rigging were in such a state that it could hardly have gone further.

The ship was just a few yards from landing when two men suddenly appeared on deck. One at the bow, the other at the stern, each threw a rope to the wharf, which the fishermen hurried to securely moor. An instinctive and ancestral gesture of welcome, which seals the solidarity between sailors of all eras and all nations.

Footbridges were thrown down, then consolidated in turn, to connect the rail and the mainland. Then, hatches were opened on the deck, and a multitude of armed men suddenly sprang from the bowels of the ship.

The inhabitants were dumbfounded and retreated in panic.

As the soldiers took possession of the wharf and secured a wide perimeter around the footbridges, an imposing silhouette appeared on the deck. With short, grey hair, shining armour, broad shoulders and a heavy blood-coloured coat, the newcomer was obviously the commander of the ship that had just docked. With a frowned brow, he watched the work in progress below. When the tumult had subsided, he calmly descended to earth, his heavy footsteps pounding the wood of the gangway in cadence. When he touched the ground, a deadly silence had fallen over the city.

The man in the purple cloak gazed with an arrogant gaze upon the assembled crowd and spoke :

"My name is Praxilas, and I am the general-in-chief of the occupying army. My fame is great on all the shores of the sea, for my victories have been many, and my reputation is such now that the enemy cities surrender and open their gates at my approach, that they may not have to endure my wrath.Perhaps some of you have heard of me ?"

He smiled proudly, sure to cause a stir in the audience, but nothing happened. Only questioning and silent faces answered him. Obviously, his story didn't mean anything to anyone. Slightly baffled, the great man continued :

"My ship has been badly damaged by last night's storm, and I need you to help me repair it. If all goes well, we'll leave in a few days and I'll be able to be magnanimous.If not..."

At these last words, murmurs were heard and the people of Orphalese began to stir. The threat was clear, and images of looting, carnage, and even destruction of the city scrolled in the assembled imaginations. Confronted to the growing nervousness of the people, the soldiers closed ranks, raising their hands to their weapons.

"Who's in charge of this city ?" said the general, covering the crowd. "Is there any edile, archon or magistrate

I can speak with ? The problem of accommodating my men and organizing their work must be settled as soon as possible !"

"Our edile is called Zain," said someone. "He lives in the most beautiful house overlooking the market square..."

"Let's find out immediately !" Praxilas said bluntly.

A dozen soldiers immediately formed a living wall around their leader, and the impressive delegation marched at a brisk pace towards the house of Zain, while the crowd silently moved aside as they passed.

YOUSSEF had not been back in town for days. Every morning now, he took his little bundle and set off for the day, walking at random, searching intuitively for the paths that Almustafa had travelled many years before him.

As he didn't know where he was going, new landscapes surprised him at every turn, for an ever-renewed wonder. Sometimes, after following the crest of the cliff for a long time, he would sit at the edge, his legs dangling, and get lost in creative meditations, questioning the sea on sentence structures, on a badly turned formula, on a word he was not sure of. Or else he would start climbing up uneasy paths on the mountainside, in the middle of desolate territories, blackened by ancient volcanic eruptions.

That day, he had sunk into a cedar forest, fragrant and mysterious. He was respectfully advancing between several hundred year old trees that rustling friendly as he passed.

At the bend of an overturned trunk, Youssef discovered a shady clearing, in the middle of which stood a number of granite blocks, which formed a kind of construction, a sort of rough and gigantic shelter. With its strange configuration, the disciple recognized a place that Almustafa had told him about several times. The prophet had described a point on earth of a particular complexion, where the energies of nature seemed to have met in a magical association. According to him, if the beings living there spent some time nearby, they could feel their life forces regenerated and their health improved. Ancient wild tribes, or forgotten giants, more sensitive than today's men to these mysterious telluric currents, had marked this region with the seal of sanctity by building fantastic monoliths for future generations.

Still as curious as ever, Youssef approached the entrance to the stone shelter, which was darker than night.

"Who goes there ?" shouted a voice inside.

A shaggy head suddenly rose out of the darkness, his eyes tinged with murderous madness. The surprise threw Youssef to the ground, and the old-timer reached for his heart, fearing that it had stopped for good.

"See my bald head and white beard," he articulated painfully. "I am but an old man, and mean you no harm !"

"What are you doing here ?" asked the other curtly. He was a tall, skinny boy, who seemed barely out of his teens with his deep black hair that nature had grouped together in random strands, and whose abrupt and insecure gestures denounced extreme nervousness.

"Nothing particular, to tell the truth," Youssef said, coming to his senses. "I walk, I meditate... I soak up the serenity of this thousand-year-old forest. Which is not your case, I think !"

"The time for serenity is over, senile monkey. The age of blood and iron has come to these lands, and it's no longer time to walk, but to fight. How can you talk to me about meditation when our brothers and sisters are under the chains of slavery ? Only the thirst for freedom and the lust for vengeance should keep you standing ! As far as I am concerned, they've been keeping me awake and awake for days."

"I don't understand your speech," said the disciple, shaking his head. "What is going on in your life that is causing so much violence ? Sit down and let's talk. Older people can be good counselors in learning how to lead a life, you know ? First of all, what's your name ?"

The young man was boiling on the spot, pacing nervously.

"Remember the name Karim well !" he said. "It's the name of the next liberator of Orphalese. But no more talking ! What good is your philosophy to me in the face of the armies of the marching oppressor ?"

"So Orphalese is oppressed ?"

"Aren't you aware of the drama going on in the city right now ?" asked Karim, taken aback.

"Well, I'm not," replied Youssef. "What should be happening there more than usual ?"

"By God, don't you know anything ? Where do you live ? Don't you know that a warship docked at the port five days ago ? All fit men have been requisitioned to repair it, and the soldiers are sleeping at their homes. They're behaving everywhere as if they were in a conquered country, and if we don't do something, they're going to settle down without a fight.

Youssef said nothing more, because the case was serious. He thoughtfully wiped his hand through the depths of his beard.

"Many young people have fled, like me," Karim continued. "In the forest and in the mountains. I'm going to rally them, organize them. Then we'll attack the city to drive out Praxilas."

"Praxilas, you say ?" asked the disciple, raising his eyebrow. "I know that name, who is it ?"

"The leader of the enemy," replied the young fugitive. "A general full of pride and self-importance, who thinks he's invincible. But I tell you, he has never fought a war who hasn't fought me !"

Youssef had a doubtful pout at the boy's candor :

"You seem very young to say that, and you don't have three hairs on your chin. How many battles have you fought to be so sure of yourself ?"

"None, but I have right and justice for me !"

The old man sighed.

"Right doesn't make victories, believe me. It's often the opposite, alas... Don't you have some secret weapon, which would tip the scales in your favor ?"

"Indeed I do," admitted Karim, exasperated."Since I have to tell you everything, her name is Yesmena."

"Yesmena ? That's a nice name for a weapon," smiled Youssef. "That's promising, tell me more !"

"Speak of her with respect, old monkey !" Karim shouted, pointing his blade at the disciple still down. "When I think of her, I'm in a rage, and I will be until the strangers have been thrown into the sea. That's why I can't lose !"

"Explain everything to me, maybe I can help you."

"Praxilas is staying with Zain, the edile of Orphalese. Yesmena is Zain's daughter, and my beloved. I'm going mad at the thought that that mangy dog could lay his hands on that sand flower.Several of his thugs have already assaulted women in the city."

Youssef thought for a moment, looking for the best course of action.

"And the edile, what is he doing ?" he asked.

"Nothing, as usual," Karim spat out. "He's a weak man, unable to make a courageous decision. We can't count on him.Last I heard, he even ordered the city militia to help the invaders maintain order, under the pretext of protecting the inhabitants !"

"I see," said the old man as he slowly got up. "I'll go and have a talk with him, for I am known to have a certain art of persuasion. On your side, see what you can do to channel the other runaways. But I implore you : no reckless act ! You would be swept away by the soldiers of Praxilas."

*
* *

"You have sent for me, Venerable One ?" said the young priest who was assisting the dean of the temple in his daily tasks.

The old man, whose bald skull could only be seen protruding from his work table, lifted up the head of his study, squinting his eyes. In the depths of the small black sloes, hidden by thick snow-covered bushes, glowed like a dark fire. An attentive observer might perhaps have been able to discern some malice, or some diffuse perversity.

"The situation in the city has changed radically with the arrival of the invaders, it seems," he said in an almost inaudible voice, as if for himself.

"Yes, the inhabitants are worried. They think that war is at their doorstep, and that terrible tragedies are about to happen."

"It's only an incident, which must not make us forget our priorities," the old man said angrily, flapping his trembling hand. "On the contrary, it might help us to clarify things..."

"What do you mean ?"

"This influx of armed forces into our streets is a godsend. The military don't like troublemakers, it's well known... and here a foreigner, who arrived recently, is claiming everywhere that he's a disciple of Almustafa, a notorious seditious...Doesn't he want to reopen the wounds of the past, excite the plebs, sow disorder ?"

The priest frowned, not daring to understand what his superior was getting at :

"Would you like us to report his presence to the edile Zain, so he can take the lead in case of trouble ?"

"No, that would be a waste of time. Zain is but a puppet in the hands of the general."

"So you suggest collaborating directly with the occupier, telling them where the man is hiding ?"

"Wouldn't that be our duty ? We must protect our flock, and prevent an unconscious blaster from triggering an infernal escalation of trouble that would lead to disaster !"

THE house of the edile Zain was certainly one of the largest and most luxurious in the city. General Praxilas had requisitioned it for nearly a week now, and he never tired of admiring it and walking around it, congratulating himself on his choice.

His room, situated on the first floor, opened onto an open courtyard with a pleasure pool and a fountain of white water.

This atrium was bordered by columns which formed a double promenade for the inhabitants of the house, on the ground floor and on the first floor. The pond, symbol of the wealth of Zain's family, simulated a wild waterhole where reeds and water lilies grew, and even housed ornamental fish and some frogs.

As every morning, when a still shy sun was seeping into the house, the general had leaned for a moment on the first floor railing to enjoy the soothing scenery of the artificial pond before going out to direct the repair yard of his ship.

Suddenly he saw Zain's daughter accompanying her tutor who had just arrived for the first lesson. Watching her go by was his secret morning appointment, to which he had immediately become accustomed, and which gave him increasing pleasure every day. Contemplating this second sun kept him happy for the rest of the day.

Yesmena realized, as she looked up, that the soldier

was watching her. She gave him an icy glance, along with a fleeting grin that was supposed to make him run away, and then, in spite of herself, smirked with a smile of victory when she saw him turn pale and freeze with his mouth open.

Suddenly paralyzed, he watched her move away for a long time, unable to take his eyes off her. Her slender figure, her feminine gait, her long dark hair carelessly brought back in a semblance of a bun, everything contributed to her natural, incomparable beauty. It was only long after she disappeared to another part of the house that he began to come to his senses.

Pierced by this vision, the General returned to his room and let himself fall on his bed. Not feeling his heartbeat, he reached his hand to his chest with concern. The turmoil lasted only for a moment, then a smile appeared on the lips of the warrior who, moments ago, thought he had a soul of metal. Was this what it was like, falling in love ? Could it be that he had never felt such a feeling before ? What was so unique about that girl that bewitched him ?

*
* *

It was then with unusual lightness that Praxilas rushed towards the harbour that morning, almost whistling his way to the dry dock where his ship was in dry dock. He had forced his close guard, who were to protect him in the streets of Orphalese, an environment which he considered hostile, where danger could arise at any moment.

Fortune had smiled upon him because, as he had hoped, he had been able to catch up with his host Zain, who had also left for the construction site shortly before.

"Good morning, edile," said the general. "I hope my presence doesn't disturb the routine of your house..."

Zain squinted his eyes into an affable smile :

"Not at all, General," he said. "It may be a small inconvenience to my staff, but it is transitory. And as you know, I do everything to keep it as short as possible. That's why I want to supervise the work on your ship myself, so that they suffer no delay..."

"I know that, my dear Zain, and I am grateful to you. I haven't arrived for a long time, but I must say that I already love your beautiful city !I have the feeling that it's a good place to live... and I certainly have nothing to complain about your welcome, nor that of your inhabitants !"

"We are a crossroads of trade and exchange, and our friendliness is renowned to the far sides of the world..."

"Aren't you suffering too much from the consequences of the war ? I have seen no after-effects in your streets and shops !"

"Divine grace has kept us from this scourge, and I pray that it will continue to be so for a long time to come..."

The invader pinched his lips.

"Alas," replied Praxilas, "I wish that misfortune would remain forever far from your shores, but I fear for your future. If for years the battles have been far from here, they are now drawing nearer.I am only the vanguard of a huge armada, and soon you will have to choose sides."

"If you love our city so much, you will protect it by maintaining its neutrality," suggested the edile with irony.

"I'm afraid that's beyond my power," concluded the other in all seriousness.

The two men continued to walk in silence for a moment.

"A most original idea has come to me," suddenly dared the soldier, "that could give Orphalese a special status, and protect her from the coming fighting !"

"Tell me, General..."

"I've lived near your daughter since I arrived at your house. She's certainly the most beautiful and charming young woman imaginable.And it seems to me that I am paid back : I feel a nascent inclination between us that only wants to grow stronger."

On hearing this, Zain frowned, because he knew his daughter, and this sudden romance did not sound like her. He couldn't imagine her at all falling for such an old man, and an enemy of the city too !

"I could marry her," Praxilas said,"and take her to live in our capital. "We are a crossroads of trade and exchange, and our friendliness is renowned to the ends of the earth..."

"Aren't you suffering too much from the consequences of the war ? I have seen no after-effects in your streets and shops !"

"Divine grace has kept us from this scourge, and I pray that it will continue to be so for a long time to come..."

The invader pinched his lips. "Alas," replied Praxilas, "I wish that misfortune would remain forever far from your shores, but I fear for your future. If for years the battles have been far from here, they are now drawing nearer.I am only the vanguard of a huge armada, and soon you will have to choose sides."

"If you love our city so much, you will protect it by maintaining its neutrality," suggested the edile with irony.

"I'm afraid that's beyond my power," concluded the other in all seriousness.

The two men continued to walk in silence for a moment.

"A most original idea has come to me," suddenly dared the soldier, "that could give Orphalese a special status, and protect it from the coming battles !"

"Tell me, General..."

"I've been with your daughter since I arrived at your house. She's certainly the most beautiful and charming young woman imaginable. And it seems to me that I am paid back : I feel a nascent inclination between us that only wishes to grow stronger."

On hearing this, Zain frowned, because he knew his daughter, and this sudden bluette did not sound like him. He couldn't imagine her at all falling for such an old man, and an enemy of the city too !

"I could marry her," Praxilas said, "and take her to live in our capital. There she would have the status of a queen !This family union would mark a wider political agreement between Orphalese and the empire, giving your city a prominent place as a protected, and therefore vital, commercial crossroads in this part of the world !"

Surprised by this unexpected proposal, Yesmena's father suddenly stopped walking. At first unsettled, the political tactician that he was quickly regained his confidence. He spent a few moments slowly rubbing his cheeks, lost in thought, trying to measure the ins and outs of the paths that were opening up in his sinuous mind, on which his daughter's destiny finally held little place.

"It is an interesting offer, which deserves to be studied carefully," he finally said.

The edile and the general shook hands before joining their respective teams, as if to seal a future agreement in advance.

AFTER his meeting with Karim in the mountains, Youssef had wanted to return to Orphalese as soon as possible, because he sensed that serious events were about to happen. But his weak strength prevented him from moving quickly, and it was only the next day that he was able to reach the market square, from where he hoped to meet the edile.

Passers-by told him that since the arrival of the soldiers, Zain had been spending all his days in the harbour, and it was there, in fact, that the disciple finally found him, lecturing carpenters about the quality of their work.

"Are you a disciple of Almustafa ?" exclaimed the edile once the disciple had introduced himself. "That's the spirit ! Perhaps you can help me, it seems that your prophet was often good advice. Look at the quagmire that existence has brought me into ! Who can tell me the right path to take ? Is there even one in a situation like this ? I'm not usually in the easiest position to be in. But nothing has prepared me for such an ordeal..."

The edile invited his visitor to sit down under a large curtain, for the sun's rays were beginning to become incisive, and then served him a cup of wine before resuming :

"When I was young, society was better structured, and people better educated. Everything was so much simpler... We lived in blessed times when the people had a blind trust in the spheres of power that guided them. These spheres were reduced to four, each represented by an eminent figure of the city : the edile, of course, representing politics, the priest for religion, the doctor for health, the schoolmaster for education. They all enjoyed an aura of immeasurable wisdom and knowledge, which no one would have doubted, and which made them untouchable. Those who knew led those who did not, and their opinions were never discussed. Yes, in truth, it was easy to govern then...

Faith and politics are the pillars of the world. They have always been, whether allying or fighting each other. But the authority of the Venerable One, in the temple, is passing away. What will happen when he's gone, before long no doubt ? The people believe less and less and have no morality ; they wander blindly, guided only by entertainment and easy pleasures.

In these dark days when everything is falling apart, when the world is turning upside down and the end of time has never seemed so near, nothing is as it was before. Youth dreams of barbarism and revolt, and no longer listens to its elders.

Myself, who sacrificed my existence to the weight of this office, I am no longer respected, and my word is constantly called into question. And yet, I no longer count the successive mandates for which the inhabitants have renewed their trust in me, nor the number of years during which I have watched over Orphalese's destiny. Today, however, my authority is being questioned for the slightest decision, so that nothing is moving forward in the affairs of the city. I am accused of corruption, inertia, nepotism. Do they think it's an easy position ? Do they think they'd do better if they had the power ? I'm telling you, friend, it would be anarchy and bankruptcy in less than three months ! It would be the end of our beautiful city !

And this judicial obsession : at the slightest dispute, we

ask for the arbitration of justice in order to obtain as much compensation as possible. In the event of an accident, you need a scapegoat to mow down in order to get the maximum amount of money out of it, so no one decides anything anymore, for fear of being brought before the judge !"

Youssef, out of courtesy, had let the edile pour out his bile, but the urgency of the situation obliged him to speed up the course of the conversation :

"There is a matter of concern that we must address urgently," he cut, "that would make the current situation much more tragic. It seems that many young people have fled into the mountains when the invaders arrived, and are preparing violent actions to drive them out of the city and back into the sea.I met the man who claims to be their leader, a man named Karim, and I asked him not to attempt anything until I had spoken to you."

"Karim ? I think I know what motivates him," Zain replied. "I've already seen him hanging around my daughter, and I've forbidden him to come near my house. He's a slacker, a good-for-nothing. His only ambition in life is to seduce an heiress from a good family who would provide him with an income so that he can bask. I can't imagine him as an anarchist, leading a revolt with arms in hand... He has neither charisma nor willpower !"

"You're probably right, but he seemed determined when I met him. What if your daughter's love gave him wings and pushed him to reckless acts ?What could you do to stop him from marching on the city, from attacking the soldiers ?"

"I don't believe it for a second, he's a coward. Besides, it would be sheer madness, his band of jokers would be wiped out in an instant. I, for one, am doing my best to guarantee the safety of the inhabitants. No doubt some people are accusing me of collaborating with the enemy ? I want you to know that I'm acting discreetly for the good of the community. Praxilas is a man of honour, and I am sure he will leave when his boat is repaired; everyone will then see that I was right to choose the path of diplomacy.I'm negotiating an agreement with him that will bind our families, and he can do no more harm to this city !"

Youssef widened his eyes, not daring to understand :

"You're not thinking of giving your daughter to him to buy peace ?"

The edile erased the remark with a wave of his hand. "I know what I have to do," he annoyed. "You don't have to know the terms of the bargain."

"But what if Karim gets his way, provoking, in retaliation, the arrival of other ships in droves ? What if the city is overwhelmed by the number of invaders, and eventually conquered ?"

The disciple was beginning to understand that Zain would not be easy to convince of the need to act quickly. Yet, who else but the edile could prevent Karim from committing the irreparable by setting off an infernal cycle of massacres and revenge ?

*
* *

Throughout the day, Praxilas multiplied the inspection rounds at the ship's repair yard. His mere presence, and his barking orders, seemed to multiply tenfold the energy of the men as he approached. The crews worked to exhaustion, and the work went on into the night by torchlight.

The general had not expected things to go so fast, and he welcomed Zain's help in convincing the people of Orphalese to participate actively and effectively. No bellicose action against his men was to be deplored. It was obviously hoped that they would leave soon, and they did not want to delay their departure at any cost. For his part, Praxilas knew he was too weak to conquer the city and impose his law by force of arms. His meagre troops would have been annihilated by a massive popular revolt. He was therefore happy that the restoration of the ship was almost complete.

Moreover, he found himself thinking more and more often about the beautiful Yesmena, and all that they could do together if he brought her back in his luggage. This delightful prospect was not for nothing in his eagerness to finish the work, nor in his concern to spare his father.

His second lieutenant came to disturb him in his reverie, accompanied by a man with a shaved head, dressed entirely in white :

"Forgive me, but I'm afraid I'm the bearer of bad news," said the soldier. "This priest has come to warn us of a stranger in town with a reputation as a troublemaker, who arrived a short while ago..."

"See there," the priest replied, holding out an inquisitive index finger. "This is the vagabond who has been talking with our edile for a long time, and who seems to want to gain influence over him."

"It's curious, it seems that his face is not unknown to me," Praxilas thoughtfully whispered.

"This is Youssef, one of Almustafa's closest companions, whom he followed to the end. We are convinced that he is not here by chance. The spirits of the inhabitants will soon be warmed by his calls for revolt..."

The general's gaze darkened as he stared at the canopy under which Zain and the bearded man seemed caught up in a lively conversation.

"We will never be rid of this fanatical plague," he whispered, clenching his teeth. "I tell you, lieutenant, the tongue of Almustafa's followers is a more dangerous weapon than an elite legion. Wherever they go, they stir up the people, turn simple souls against us, and sedition spreads like fire through the bushes. Stop that one ! And discreetly, for God's sake, I don't want any trouble."

YOUSSEF and Zain had spoken for a long time, and the night was already very late when they parted. The old man didn't have the courage to climb back up the cliff to his shack and went to Almitra's house, where he was sure he would not be refused lodging.

"There he is ! It's him, I recognize him !"

In the faint glow of the blaze, Youssef saw a soldier pointing at him.

By reflex, he rushed back into the alley where he came from. He started running as fast as his weary knuckles would allow him, and managed to squat painfully in a dark corner, at the bottom of a perpendicular alleyway, before the troop had time to emerge at his height. Breathless, his eyes full of panic rolling in all directions, he tried to pierce the darkness while hoping to melt into it to disappear.

"Youssef of Pyrimar ! You are under arrest ! Surrender !"

How many times had he dreaded hearing this terrible phrase, which resounded against the walls of the deserted city ? Covered in a tangle of chicken cages and hutches, terrorized, compelling himself to the most perfect immobility, the old man was brutally plunged back into the most terrible moments of the manhunt that had followed the execution of Almustafa, targeting all his close followers. More than once, he had escaped only by a miracle.

The lost years passed in his memory. All his travels,

the countless encounters... All those faces, those welcoming glances, those shared laughter and tears... So many friendships were born along those roads.

But what if, under the guise of spreading the word of the prophet, he had only been running away all this time ? Running further and further away, as the threat advanced ? What if he was just a coward, wearing the oversized toggles of a junk wise man, a ridiculous lecturer unable to follow the path he advocated ?

And always this inner dialogue that came back to poison him, rocking him with sweet lies to comfort him in his choices :

"If I'm arrested, if I die, who will bear witness to what I've seen ? Who will be able to pick up the torch and pass on the words of Almustafa ? But if I go to bed again, if I hide and run away, how can I still have any self-respect, how can I claim to be worthy of the Beloved ? He who has never trembled at the threat, and has always walked, on all roads, under cheers and booing, with equal steps ?"

Suddenly, another voice was heard : "Let go, my brother, and never know fear again ! Trust in Life ! Not one iota of what you do in its name can be taken away from you..."

It was that of the Prophet, which resounded in his mind as if whispered in his ear.

"How can I still be plagued by doubt ?" Youssef thought.

He stood up, and came out of his hiding place with a new resolution. Perhaps he had lived as a coward all his life, but he would die with the courage of his convictions. He went out into the light, into the main street, and walked towards the soldiers.

"Don't look for me anymore, I'm here," he said simply. "Do what you have to do..."

THE city of Orphalese was not known for the cruelty of its justice, nor the insalubrity of its jails. However, these did not depart from the rules of security and discipline inherent to their function. Thus, it was indeed a heavy iron screen door that closed creaking behind Youssef, blocking with a noise of lock and chain any passage to freedom.

The cell that he was discovering, which contained only a thin straw mattress and a stool, was certainly no less comfortable than his hovel in the four winds on the cliff... but, precisely, he was missing the four winds and the cliff.

The eternal pilgrim took three steps in one direction, two steps in the other, and thought that in such a cage it would not take him long to wither and wish for death. Would he even have time to do so ?

He thought about his surrender. Was it really an act of bravery, or had he reached the end of the road anyway ? Hadn't his endless march, his fleeing, muddled itself, hadn't it blindly reached a dead end ?

Raising his head towards an opening in the wall that let the moonlight shine through, he saw that the thickness of the wall would prevent him from seeing the sky. He then let himself fall on his mattress and took his head in his hands. Ah ! If he had been able to write at least... Yes, writing might have saved him, but he remembered the calames he had left up there, and thought that he would probably never again be able to caress them lovingly...

He wouldn't be able to carry out the last mission he'd set himself. Bitter tears streamed down his twisted and trembling palms.

*
* *

That same night, other hands, mysterious hands, traced a message in red paint on several façades of the city, which, making a strange amalgam, was unambiguously intended for the invaders :

"Long live free Orphalese ! Long live Almustafa, our saviour !"

*
* *

At the first lights of dawn, the door of the cell opened with a bang, allowing General Praxilas to pass through. Grabbing the stool, he sat down facing Youssef, who had not moved all night. Like a cat that wants to play with its prey, with a sly smile, he stared at the emaciated face of the disciple for a long time, lingering on the sunken cheeks, the deep furrows in the forehead, the dark circles under the eyes, the long shaggy beard.

"I know you, Youssef of Pyrimar," he said at last. "For some years now, your name has resounded in many coastal towns. On all the shores, people have seen you, they have listened to your stories of old fools. There is not a country where your honeyed speech hasn't captivated some simple soul, and the faithful of Almustafa are numberless. Or should I say the followers of your sect ?"

"Now that I see you better, I recognize you, General. How ironic to find you again, twenty years after the tragic events that made me an orphan and a wanderer."

"Did you consider Almustafa your father ?" Praxilas asked.

"As a brother, and as a father, yes. He had opened my eyes to a new way of looking at life, and truly I was born again following in his footsteps. He had delivered me to myself, sort of speak... revealed, to my own eyes, who I really was."

"Beautiful words, which hide lies and perfidy... What I see is agitation and turmoil, revolt and sedition, hundreds of deaths. These were the words of your master, and they still stir when their last embers are rekindled by the pitiful survivors of your kind."

He grabbed the old man's chin in his hand, pushing his nails into his gaunt cheeks, forcing him to look at him :

"But this time I got you, you fanatical scum, and your cursed tongue will never again be able to distill its venom ! Yes, I was there when your master was put to death. Yes, it was I who gave the order, and I will not rest until I have completed the work. You and your kind are a cancer, which grows back more vigorously when a head is cut off, and spreads as soon as it is attacked. But I am the doctor, the potion, the cautery, and I will wipe you from the face of the earth..."

And it was like madness spitting from his eyeballs.

THE memory of the Prophet was still alive in the minds of the people of Orphalese, and his words of wisdom, full of peace, were still often heard in conversations. For this reason, there was great incomprehension when it was learned that one of his closest followers had been imprisoned by the invaders. The matter was much discussed and people began to gather in small groups, in which agitation and then anger grew. Everyone saw this as an arbitrary act, an abdication of the edile in favor of the occupying forces, and further proof that the city was no longer in control of its destiny.

Spontaneous demonstrations demanding Youssef's release moved towards the house of Zain, which had become the symbol of oppression. But after a few minutes of agitation, several dozen men in arms and uniforms rushed to the square and established a protective cordon around the building. They were the municipal militia, a kind of local police force that usually kept order in the streets of Orphalese. Created at the instigation of Zain, it was largely financed out of his personal fortune, and one could legitimately doubt its objectivity in some of its interventions. For this time, in any case, it was clear that it was not on the side of the people !

So for several hours, fists were raised under close surveillance, and voices shouted under the balconies of the edile who didn't deign to show his face.

Finally, a large contingent of Praxilas soldiers came to lend a hand to the militiamen, and invaded the place where the people had gathered, blocking all the exits. Formed in successive lines, swords drawn, shields raised, visors lowered revealing only clenched jaws, they had the delicate task of dispersing the demonstrators without shedding blood, which meant that they could only count on intimidation. But they knew from experience that, in the heat of the late afternoon, all the ingredients were in place for the slightest spark on either side to cause a drama.

Fortunately, their patibular mines, made even more frightening by their panoply of metal, were enough this time to calm the spirits, and the demonstrators dispersed grumbling to avoid a massacre foretold. The fear of the troop and its violence still made it possible to maintain order, and by a miracle no incident was to be deplored, except for a few stone throws against the soldiers, who had managed to keep their nerves. But how long could this precarious balance last ? The fact that the militia and the foreigners were working together confirmed the worst suspicions : Zain had delivered the city to Praxilas, and was collaborating shamelessly.

As the days passed, the unrest soon changed shape, and it was at night that the protest began to take shape.

At first they were messages of insult against Praxilas and his henchmen, which were traced on the walls of the administrative buildings. They were added to the mysterious red messages invoking Almustafa, and each night more of them were added.

The graffiti was soon followed by violent acts, and small groups attacked the symbols of the occupying army, attacking isolated soldiers and committing sabotage in the shipyard.

Repairs to the ship weren't complete, and she was still unable to return to sea. Praxilas watched with concern as his hold on the city diminished day by day. Soon Orphalesis would realize the weakness of his forces, and everything would change. So he decided to play his part.

On the third morning of tensions, an edict was posted in all public places announcing the promulgation of martial law.At sunset, the inhabitants of Orphalese would have to lock themselves in their homes and not come out until the next morning.

At nightfall, the alleys would be frequented only by the troop that would methodically criss-cross the city to prevent any popular unrest.

The day after the promulgation, the general did not notice any particular reaction in the city, and he was reassured. But when he went to the docks, he immediately saw that the number of workers had dramatically decreased. In fact, there were only a few old men who were not very efficient.By the end of the morning, the many reports he had received were consistent : the vast majority of young people had deserted Orphalese.

And that was definitely not a good sign...

THE cell was lit only by a small barred skylight, placed at a height inaccessible to the prisoners. Facing it, Youssef was sitting on the floor, prey to dark thoughts. The sun was setting outside, and soon he would be plunged into total darkness. The disciple wanted to take advantage of the last light of dusk, wondering what the next day would bring.

Strange noises above him, rubbing, sliding, brought him out of his torpor :

"Who's there ?" he shouted anxiously, straightening up.

"Silence !" a voice blew from outside. "Do you want to get us killed ?"

A dark figure quickly passed behind the bars.

"Who are you ? What do you want ?" Youssef resumed in fear.

"Hey, old man, you still alive ? Haven't the rats eaten you yet ?"

In the mocking tone of the interjection, the disciple recognized little Mustapha. He sighed with relief, for he believed that Praxilas was quite capable of sending assassins to make him disappear discreetly from the face of the Earth.

"Are you on the roof ? How did you get up there ?"

"I'm resourceful ! Besides, I bring you some comfort

from my mother..."

The child slid a small leather purse through the bars, attached to a string that he quickly untied. The old man grabbed it, and opened it without further ado. He found bread and cheese, and a small flask that must have contained wine.

"Enough to keep you in shape," said Mustapha. "Unfortunately, I don't have the means to get you out of here."

Starving, the old man began to devour what was being sent to him.

"So, what news ?" he articulated between two bites. "How's Almitra ?"

"She's fine, but she's worried about you."

"Tell her I'll be all right, I've seen others..."

"In the city, on the other hand, things are bad. The people are getting restless, and it's fair to say you've made a big mess !"

"How could I ? Nobody knows me !"

""Strange things have been happening, though, since you've been here. Even graffiti in the name of Almustafa is growing on the walls !"

"What ? ! It doesn't make any sense. Why involve the Master in all this ?"

"I don't know who's behind the scene, but your arrest has sparked riots, which have angered Praxilas. He's now imposing martial law and a curfew which deprives us of our liberties."

The old disciple scratched his forehead, taking a few moments of reflection to untangle the situation, which was going crazy.

"It's beyond me," he finally admitted. "I think they're trying to smear the name of the Prophet, but I don't know to what end. I do note, however, that the curfew is not too much of an obstacle to your movements !"

"I'm not the kind of bird that is kept in a cage..."

Now satisfied, the old traveller had come to his senses, and other preoccupations came to his mind :

"Listen, Mustapha, Providence has sent you. Something very serious is going on, more urgent than all the rest. You absolutely must warn your mother..."

"More serious than the invasion of Orphalese by foreign troops ? And the curfew ?"

"Some young people are hiding in the mountains, and I met their leader by chance. They plan to attack the city to eliminate the soldiers, or throw them into the sea !"

"Rich idea ! Who's in charge ?"

"He told me his name was Karim, but I understood that he knew nothing about command or war..."

"Karim ? I know him, he's a fool ! He'll never make it !"

"Do you believe me when I tell you that he's capable of the worst madness ?"

"I do..."

"I'm afraid they'll be massacred, and a lot of people with them. I've warned the edile Zain, but I'm not sure he'll do much. Take cover, get out of town before it's too late !"

*

* *

As the darkness was gathering outside, everyone felt that terrible trials were about to strike the city, and a foretaste of the end of the world hovered in the silent streets and entered the houses.

Almitra could not escape this deleterious atmosphere, which had found refuge in her belly in the form of a ball of anguish that never left her side. She held in her hands a perfectly polished copper disc, a mirror that faithfully reflected the image of the old woman she had become. For hours, she had been scrutinizing her features, without complacency, trying to read in her own eyes the answers to her questions, counting in the grooves that marked her the balance of her past life.

What had she done during all these years ? Had she at all times expressed the highest part of herself ? Had she always done her best, participated in the improvement of the life of her contemporaries, in all its aspects ? Did she share the light she had received ? In a word, had she been faithful to the teachings of Almustafa ?

She often wondered why she had not followed him when he had left Orphalese. And later, when her fame was growing on the other side of the sea, what had she not joined him ? Would he have chosen her among his disciples ? She did not doubt it. What would she have done then, in the last moments, when the dark forces forced the Light to extinguish, tried to tarnish the brilliance of her words by covering them with opprobrium, destroyed the most beautiful gift of Life in the world ? Would it have blocked his body, fighting tooth and nail to protect it ? Would she have died bravely at his side, without ever denying his ideals ? Or would she have been like the majority, fearful and elusive, suddenly disappearing into the comforting anonymity of the crowd ?

Instead of this life of adventure, she had chosen to start a family, to have a child. The battle between her mind and her entrails had turned sour, the spirit had, from the start,

100

no chance. Until then, she had never regretted this path of life. But, unexpectedly, the latest events brought up the dilemmas of the past.

"Here come the dark days of the hunt again," she thought to herself. "The past returns knocking at your door, and the threat that we thought was forever gone is suddenly within our walls. All our friends will be hunted down and put out of business. How will you react ? Will you stand up to the oppressor ? Or will you try to disappear like a rabbit in his burrow, waiting for the danger to pass ?"

She remembered what the Prophet said about what awaited those who would follow him, or would like to express his truth.

"The more you allow the Divine Consciousness to penetrate your life, and change its tone, the stranger your behavior, your words, your way of being, will seem to your contemporaries. For as your impregnation increases, the need to express the divinity within you in every way will become irrepressible.

In time, your priorities will change. You will need less and less of their gaze, of their assent to be happy. Their contempt will become more and more vivid, their criticisms more and more sharp, but will no longer touch you. They will laugh at you, make fun of your words, your clothes, your food.

You will want to talk about the sun to those who have always lived in a cave, and they will hate you for it.

Because of what I have taught you, you will be called mad, molested, and cast out of the cities. You will be driven to solitude, but you will not care, for you will be filled with all your discoveries, and your dialogue with the Universe will be less and less interrupted.

And when you finally believe yourself to be at peace, moments of discomfort will present themselves to you again, pushing you into your final entrenchments again and again, in order to pass your soul through the rolling mill, to remove chip after chip all that is not necessary, and to bring to light little by little the precious gem that is hidden in the gangue of your heart of stone..."

The door of the house opened abruptly, and little Mustapha entered in a gust of wind, as usual.

"They're going to attack the town !" he managed to articulate out of breath. "They want to throw the soldiers back into the sea !"

Undoubtedly, a moment of discomfort presented itself...

When her son had summed up the situation, Almitra stood up slowly. She had never been so pale before. It was clear to her now that the time had come to act :

"I have to go and talk to Karim tonight ! I'll dissuade him from his foolish enterprise before he commits the irreparable."

"But how are you going to do that, with the curfew ?"

She looked at her son with a seriousness he didn't know she had :

"I'm going to need you and your friends. Can you warn them, and tell them to gather here as soon as possible ?"

"Consider it done, they can't be far !"

The young boy left the house as quickly as he had entered.

Almitra planned to use her son's band of friends to distract the soldiers guarding the exit of the town, while she would quietly run away. It cost her to endanger her own flesh and blood in this way. But in the dark hours they were going through, she saw no other solution.

With the unconsciousness of youth, Mustapha had accepted, of course. All this was just another game, a new chance to break the daily routine, and to live an adventure with his friends.

Less than an hour later, a dozen or so children were gathered at the home of the temple's former seer, and a plan was soon devised that would allow her to leave Orphalese unhindered by darkness.

It was very late at night when the rascal troop left the house, a few minutes ahead of Almitra. Their strategy was well thought out, as they had already tried it many times before, for bad jokes or petty theft of little importance. This time, however, they would be up against professional soldiers, in a state of extreme nervousness, who would have no qualms if they caught them. The little conspirators evaporated silently in the alleys, with a mixture of excitement and apprehension in their stomachs. Everyone would take action at the agreed signal, once they had all come close to the city gate that opened onto the mountain.

Promoted leader of the band for this special mission, Mustapha was the first to arrive at the Great Gate of the East. Sneaking on the crest of a roof, he risked a glance towards the ramparts. Luckily, only two sentries were on duty this time. They could easily be scattered !

It has always been universally recognized that the cry of the tawny owl is the signal for action. So the children knew exactly what they had to do when they heard it ringing over the rooftops. They grabbed their slings and carefully adjusted the head of the nearest soldier, whose helmet shone dimly in the moonlight.

The first shot hit the target, and the man swore, more surprised than hurt. He did not have time to understand what was happening to him when a shower of small round stones, carefully chosen, began to hit him all over his body with diabolical precision. As he stepped back to take cover, the other guard looked for the aggressors, trying to pierce the darkness above the houses that surrounded him.

Suddenly the attack ceased, and then a cavalcade sound was heard at the other end of the street. The soldiers were stung to the core, and rushed out of their posts, drawing their swords and leaving their posts without further thought.

As they went off in pursuit of the children, Almitra slipped through the heavy gate that protected the city. She knew she had only a few minutes to get far enough away and take cover, so she hurried to the first groves, trying to make as little noise as possible.

In the end, everything had gone as smoothly as possible.She prayed a quick prayer for her son and the other boys, who had taken all the risks and were not yet out of danger, before going into the night to attack the first foothills, on paths that only hunters and healers in search of medicinal plants knew.

Part III

Yesmena

MUSTAPHA had been playing with the guards for almost an hour. Always invisible, he was driving them crazy by throwing pieces of tiles at them, then suddenly changing streets by jumping from roof to roof, climbing up terraces or playing tightrope walker on the edge of a low wall.

But he was getting tired, and thought that his mission, to give his mother time to get away, was largely accomplished.

So he was about to go home when, near a small square, he witnessed a strange activity, which might have seemed less suspicious had it not been at night.

Many Praxilas soldiers were there, silently busy mounting motley piles of sandbags, sticks, pieces of palisades... But what were they doing ? Certainly nothing good for the people of Orphalese.

Frustrated not to be able to see any more, he climbed up to the nearest roof and stood up, forgetting all caution, just as the moon was coming out of the clouds.

"There he is, I see him !" screamed a voice behind him below. "This time we've got him !"

Mustapha cursed his curiosity and resumed his acrobatic cavalcade. But lassitude and darkness got the better of his skill, and his foot stumbled against two disjointed tiles. Unbalanced, he slumped all the way down and tumbled down the slope without being able to restrain himself, until he fell into the void.

During the two seconds it took him to fall, he felt like he was dying... but luckily he was cushioned by a pile of baskets and bundles and came out of the fall without a scratch.

Recovering, the young boy realized that he had fallen into a tiny courtyard, made even more cramped by the unbelievable pile of bags and accessories, paint buckets, vases and pots that piled up randomly in uncertain colonnades, until he reached the overhanging balconies. Probably the storeroom of some kind of shop...

Alarmed by the din, a man put his head through a doorway leading to the courtyard :

"Welcome to Alhena and Munir's house, boy," he whispered, not afraid, and even less angry. "What brings you, at this hour, to the best potters in the country ?"

On the street, however, the excitement of the guards was at its peak. After banging on the door for a few moments, they broke it down and rushed into the shop.

Alarmed, Alhena had barely had time to get dressed and leave her room, only to find herself surrounded by the men-at-arms, without understanding what was going on.

"A fugitive is hiding in your house," shouted one of the soldiers, grabbing her violently by the arm. "Give him to us, or we'll arrest you in his place !"

He shook her mercilessly.

"I don't know what you're talking about !" she shouted back. "Let go of me !"

"He was on your roof a moment ago."

"She didn't see anything, Sir, she's blind," said another, laughing.

"If that's the way it is, we'll search it ourselves," replied the officer.

He hit Alhena in the face, and she collapsed among the vases and plates, breaking many of her precious creations.

Enraged by the prolonged stalking, the men began to smash everything in the shop, then entered the workshop.

"So, bitch, what are you hiding behind that curtain, huh ?"

The chief moved backwards.

"What the hell is that ?"

The spectacle that awaited them froze them in horror. A deformed cripple was rolling around at their feet, foaming at the mouth and screaming like a demon.

They retreated sharply as the poor, swarming creature tried to grab their legs with demented glances.

"He is afflicted with grand mal," said one of the soldiers in a white voice. "Whoever touches him will be cursed !"

The little troop walked away as one man, suddenly cooled down.

"The fugitive can't be here," the officer suddenly decided after a quick circular sweep of the workshop.

The soldiers came out of the shop in disorder, as hastily as they had entered.

After waiting a few minutes for the nightly silence to return to the street, Mustapha came out of his hiding place and rushed towards Alhéna who was still lying in the pottery debris.

Munir also arrived from the workshop, happy with the trick he had played on the invaders. It's so easy, when you're handicapped, to frighten simple souls !

But his smile disappeared when he saw his sister, who was barely able to stand up. Her face swollen, her lip open, she had hurt herself in many places by falling on the shards.

Still shocked by what had just happened, conscious that they had narrowly escaped much more serious torments, the three of them hugged each other for a long time, without uttering a word.

It was Alhena who broke the silence :

"Stay with us until morning, you'll be safe."

Mustapha nodded.

MEANWHILE, in the night made impenetrable by the thickness of the forest, Almitra was advancing much slower than she had hoped. She thought her knowledge of the paths would compensate for the lack of visibility, but it was not so. More than ten times she thought she was lost for good, until, by some miracle, she finally emerged from the foliage and saw the chalk slopes gleaming under the moon, pointing her in the right direction.

She allowed herself a few moments of respite to catch her breath, listening to the strange sounds of the nocturnal animals of the mountain, still fearing that she had been followed. Then, taking her courage in both hands, she began the most difficult part of her ascent.

In her haste, she had taken only a stole to protect herself from the cold, and no matter how tightly she held it, the piece of cloth proved to be insufficient, even as the coldest hours were just beginning. As her modest sandals crumbled on the stones of the path that rolled under her weight, and as the crisp air of the altitude filled her with needles that made her shiver, she still wondered what madness had taken her. But now it was too late to turn back.

The arduous climb seemed to have lasted forever, when suddenly, at the end of a loop, she saw the glow of lights slightly below. As she had sensed, Karim had chosen a place full of magic and history to set up his bivouac. It was easy for him to lure the fugitives there, for it was a place known to all the inhabitants of Orphalese, where the remains of an ancient civilization, perhaps giants, lay. They had been the first to inhabit these places from time immemorial, and all that remained of their fantastic constructions were a few raised stones decorated with engravings, as well as immense heads that had fallen to the ground, broken, mutilated, half buried in the earth.

As she approached, her eyes widened before the dimensions of the camp which the fugitives had hastily built. How many of them were there ? There were several dozen tents, and a multitude seemed to be stirring in the improvised alleys.

Established on a high plateau, on the other side of the mountain, the installations of the maquisards were invisible from the city. Convinced that they were safe, and especially because of their inexperience, they had not posted guards, and Almitra was able to walk among the rough shelters without being arrested. The small groups she passed through, in the midst of which she passed like a ghost, seemed to have just come out of childhood, and gave the impression that it was all a game. We laughed, we chased each other, we hugged each other, because many of the girls had left their families, out of love or conviction. Everywhere there was improvisation and disorder. This little world was so engrossed in the preparations for the upcoming battle that no questions were asked. She had the nerve to ask where Karim was and, to her surprise, she was shown to his tent without further ado. She entered it with a determined step, invested with all her will to convince.

Karim was there, eating. Softly slumped to a semblance of a table, he carelessly swallowed a few grapes, seemingly totally indifferent to the hustle and bustle around him. When he recognized his unexpected host, he stood up respectfully :

"You are Almitra, aren't you, the soothsayer of the temple ?" he said, handing her a cup of wine he had just filled.

She accepted it gratefully, for she was at the end of her strength. Everyone knew and loved her, and she had become, in time, one of the notables of the city, if not by power, then by heart. So with all due respect, he invited her to sit down and eat.

She spoke without delay, for the sun was about to rise :

"I remember the time when your mother used to bring you to the temple, so that I could counsel her about you. She didn't know what to do with you, because you were already doing as you pleased..."

"I remember it too, a little... Your clairvoyant powers were renowned throughout the region and beyond. But you didn't see what's been going on in the city for the past few weeks, it seems to me."

"In my defense, I long ago retired from the turpitudes of society. But you're right, I didn't foresee one of our children endangering all the others with his egomaniacal insanity. I know your plans, and I have come to dissuade you from them : you are running to your doom, and you are taking our youth to certain death !"

Karim burst out laughing :

"You talked to old Youssef, didn't you ? You have the same speech ! Decidedly, you can't count on white hair to make a revolution... Of course there are risks, I'm not minimizing them. But it's not by clinging to your tranquility, your habits, your cowardice, that you'll make things happen."

"Have you ever known war ? I'm talking about the slaughter of dozens of you. You've never fought, and you want to face seasoned soldiers !"

"Some of us will be sacrificed, no doubt. But have you

considered our numbers ? We will break like the waves of the ocean on the walls of Orphalese, like the plagues of God's wrath, and nothing will be able to resist us, not even the army of Praxilas. The few survivors in their ranks will flee with their tails between their legs."

Karim paused to take a sip of wine. Then he paid attention to the rumors outside.

"When I say that Youssef is too old for fighting, I'm wrong," he said. "Even if he takes part without knowing it..."

"What do you mean ?"

"His arrival awakened the ghost of the prophet Almustafa, whom everyone in Orphalese had forgotten. Myself, I confess, was unaware of his existence until recently. However, thanks to Youssef, I could see that his memory was still very much alive around here. I asked about his history, his ideas. The elders consider him a child of the country. I understood that he was a local hero, who died as a martyr, under the blows of those who invade us today !"

"I'm afraid I understand where you're getting at..."

"So I began to have the prophet's name painted in blood on the streets, and the success exceeded my expectations !"

"You are crazy ! Almustafa was a man of peace, how dare you sully his name like this !"

"Don't you see that everything is going beautifully ? All the pieces fit together in perfection, and now you can't stop what's begun ?"

The seer's face was decomposing as the rebel unfolded his plan.

"And the best part is that the final touch was again made by Youssef, when he was arrested at just the right moment ; it was the ideal moment to set the souls on fire, and the people reacted accordingly. He is now ready to

114

support our action, because he is convinced of its merits !"

The more the young man spoke, the more Almitra boiled on the spot :

"You are unspeakably cynical ! You're a monster !" she exploded. "I thought you were an idealist, but you're a miserable upstart, trampling on the most sacred values to satisfy your thirst for power !"

"Easy, old woman ! Is this how you treat me, when you invite yourself into my home and I welcome you with open arms ?"

"If I were your mother, I'd spank you good and that'd be the end of it ! But I realize I can't change your mind... However, I invite you to think carefully about the consequences of your actions, because you can still stop everything ! And if you should know only one word of Almustafa, let it be this : *If you have a choice between death and life, choose life !*"

"I heard you, but I don't have any choice. Come on, follow me ! This is the dawn, the hour when history is made !"

He opened the sheet that covered the entrance of his tent with a brisk gesture, and threw himself out making reels with his sword. Livid, desperate, Almitra followed him, wringing her hands.

Karim climbed a collapsed monolith, on which were still some traces of engravings as old as mankind. As if the time of the rendezvous had been fixed long ago, the revolted people had already begun to gather around their leader.

After he had glanced around to gauge his troops, he suddenly pointed at Almitra with the tip of his blade as she tried to move away.

"Look at this woman," he said. "Many of you know her, if only by reputation. Her science of medicine and divination has saved many of our families. This is Almitra, the closest friend of our guide Almustafa !"

All eyes converged on the one that no one had noticed until now, and silence fell.

"She came to bring me the latest news of our brother Youssef, the closest disciple of our Beloved, unjustly imprisoned by the invaders," the young chief added. "He awaits our intervention impatiently, for he fears for his life ! Moreover Almitra blesses our action in the name of Almustafa, who always fought for freedom, and even died for it !"

Medushed, she saw all these young men suddenly going mad, frantically waving their fists in the air, waving makeshift weapons they had stolen from the city or the surrounding fields, rapiers and sickles, simple sticks or poor spikes hastily made in the camp.

When Karim felt they were warm enough, he pointed to the ocean far below :

"Follow me, children of Orphalese ! The time has come, we can wait no longer ! Let's take back what's ours ! For freedom ! For Almustafa !"

A massive clamor greeted his command, and all marched towards the city, shouting *Al-mus-ta-fa ! Al-mus-ta-fa !* .

Karim threw a last glance of triumph to the old woman, before jumping to get lost in the crowd.

"Murderer !" she blew between her teeth, as she felt tears of impotence rising.

K ARIM'S plan was simple, which he believed was the key to success. He had divided his troops into two equal sections, each entering the city through an opposite gate, one on the east and one on the west. They would then converge towards the centre of the city, the market square and the port, to surround the occupants and destroy them. Orphalese had many gates, but those chosen by the young strategist seemed the most easily accessible, as their proximity to the sea deprived them of a good defence.

The first lights of the solar disc were barely above the ocean when Karim and his vanguard arrived in sight of the ramparts overlooking the eastern gate. They watched for a moment as the sentries came and went between the battlements, gauging the distance between them and the heavy leaves that barred their access to the city, and which they would have to break through.

Not all the fighters in Karim's young army were in-experienced. Some, whom he had sent to the vanguard, were indeed excellent hunters, who handled the bow with dexterity and precision, and approached their prey with deadly discretion.

Once they had become well acquainted with the rou-tine of the guards of Praxilas, the archers silently slid towards the ramparts, and, taking advantage of the few hiding places offered by the relief of the rocky coast on the outskirts of the city, managed to position themselves almost below the enemy, within shooting distance. The aim was to eliminate the guards as quietly as possible, before they sounded the alarm.

After conferring with one another, the hunters shot their arrows simultaneously, and in an instant, three soldiers fell without a shout.

Karim waited a minute to judge the reactions behind the wall to this surprise attack, but nothing happened. They had probably neutralized all the sentries at this entrance to the city !

He then ordered his troops to run to the gates and open them as quickly as possible to take advantage of the surprise effect.

But when the first attackers reached the ramparts, they watched in horror as comrades fell behind them screaming in pain.

Two other soldiers had appeared between the battlements, trying to resist the human tide that was rushing towards them, shooting arrow after arrow at them. It took several endless seconds before Karim's archers could finally reach them and put them out of harm's way.

The rebels then gathered at the gates, and with a few loud and violent blows, broke them down with a ram they had made in the mountain from a huge trunk of a hundred-year-old cedar tree. Galvanized by these first successes, which they achieved quickly and almost without a single blow, they then rushed into the city, shouting with joy, sure of their victory. It was no longer a question of discretion, but of speed in the conquest of the city's hot spots.

But once inside, when they expected strong resistance, they met not a living soul.

Surprised, the older men in the front ranks slowed down when they saw that all the streets leading from the entrance of the city were deserted and defenseless. Could it be that a trap had been set for them ?

They did not have time to think for long, for already some spirited teenagers, confident in their lucky stars, were pushing them and overtaking them to penetrate further into Orphalese.

"Hurry up !" they shouted. "We've got them by surprise !"

Elbowing their way through the bottleneck of the gate, the swarming mass of liberators poured into Orphalese, spreading out into the street leading straight into the centre of the city.

But after a good half of the young rebels had passed through the gates, dark and threatening silhouettes suddenly appeared on the crests of the roofs of the houses that stood at the entrance to the city, and concentrated a heavy fire on the disorderly crowd that was jostling to get through.

Unable to move forward or backward, many young men were hit and left behind between the gaping doors of the East Gate, before panic finally broke out into two groups : those who had managed to enter the city ran further towards the centre for cover, while those who had remained outside the walls quickly moved away from them to be out of reach of the enemy archers.

The soldiers of Praxilas took advantage of these few moments of disorganization to close and consolidate the gates, after freeing them from the bodies that encumbered them. Going up on the ramparts, they shouted cries of victory to Karim's troops who had returned to the foot of the mountain.

They still had not understood what had just happened. Medushed by this sudden turn of events, cut off from their leader who had remained prisoner inside, they no longer knew what to do.

*
* *

After the sudden disappearance of the Orphalesian youths, Praxilas had foreseen that an attack of this kind could take place at any time. He had therefore mobilized his weak forces, aided by Zain's militia who knew the city's crucial crossing points, to barricade certain streets in record time, during the night, and establish an obligatory passage, which would contain Karim's waves of disorderly assault, and take them where he wanted them : to deadly culs-de-sacs where his men, positioned high and sheltered, could decimate them as they trained. By involving his militiamen in this macabre enterprise, the Aedile had now reached an irreversible degree in his policy of collaboration, which became complicity in crime.

The general was a fine strategist and, posted at the top of one of the highest towers of Orphalese, he had watched with delight, clapping his hands like a child, Karim's army being cut in two as it passed through the gates, somewhat restoring the balance of power.

Now he could see with morbid satisfaction the movements of the crowd of rebels trapped *intra-muros*, a vociferous and anarchic mass, following the routes he had imposed on them. Like a slimy beast, it poured into the alleys, seeking its way, dividing at each crossroads, trying to retreat when it encountered a barricade, but not being able to, pushed by the rearguard whose inertia precipitated it into the nooks and crannies from which it could no longer escape.

Most of the young men had never seen death up close, and could not imagine the horror of street fighting. The few rudimentary notions of discipline they had acquired in the mountains evaporated when the first companions fell to the ground screaming, touched by the unstoppable features from the sky.

Trapped like flocks of sheep in these naked cul-de-sacs offering no protection, they did not realize until it was too late that they had been manipulated. Turning wild glances in all directions, they suddenly forgot their anger and their thirst to fight and gave in to panic.

While most of them were desperately seeking shelter in an animal reflex, others, more seasoned, more unconscious, or simply driven out of their minds by the danger, set out to dislodge the soldiers who were slaughtering them from the rooftops. They rushed into the houses, breaking down the doors and stormed the stairs towards the terraces where their executioners had been stationed. But up there, they were awaited with a firm foot, and the narrowness of the passages that opened on the roofs allowed the swords to pick them off one by one, without the rebels being able to represent the slightest danger.

With the energy of desperation, and probably because he was the most motivated, Karim fought like a lion. Followed by a few others, he had managed to climb a barricade, and rushed downtown in search of Praxilas. Meeting little resistance at first, they easily defeated a few lightly armed militiamen. But as they progressed, the soldiers began to chase more and more of them, hitting them one after the other.

Soon there were only a handful of them left to resist,

cornered on the steps of the temple, which they gradually climbed backwards, pushed up by the joint attacks of the militia and the occupiers.

Karim drummed on the heavy doors that closed the access to the sanctuary, playing his all-purpose drum :

"Asylum !" he shouted desperately. "I demand asylum ! Save children of Orphalese threatened with death !"

On the other side of the door, some novices had tried to open it for him. But the Venerable had prevented them from doing so. They had remained there, silent, without moving, waiting for the inevitable end of the assault, only separated from the horror by the thickness of the wood.

When his last companion had fallen at his feet, Karim felt his forces abandon him. In a scream of rage, he threw down his sword and raised his hands in surrender.

Covered in blood, his body lacerated with multiple wounds, he did not protest when soldiers garroted him and dropped him to his knees, beating him. Unconscious, he was taken to the prison, in a cell close to Youssef's cell.

*

* *

It took some time after the tumult of arms had subsided for the inhabitants to dare to go outside again. The streets had suffered the harshness of the fighting, but it was impossible to measure the extent of the damage, nor the casualties among the children of Orphalese. Praxilas understood that he had narrowly escaped a catastrophe, the submergence of his troops under the number, but that it was still possible if the city was taken in a vengeful outburst of anger.

Luckily, Karim's troops who had not been able to enter the city had fled into the mountains, probably returning to their makeshift camps. But before long, perhaps they would regain their strength, and launch desperate new attacks...

For now, Orphalese was stunned, bruised. Drained of its life force, it recognized the general as its victor.So he had to move quickly to nip in the bud any hint of further rebellion, while adorning his commands with the legality of a judgment from the local authorities.

A mock trial was hastily organized, and Karim's death sentence was proclaimed in the evening by posters on all the doors of public places in Orphalese. It would be applied the next day and, under pressure from the foreign army, the judges had chosen stoning, as a reminder of the fate that would befall all the followers of Almustafa if they persevered in their fanaticism.

THE sky was low and dark when, in the early morning of the next day, Karim was brought to the place of his execution, a small deserted area under the city walls. The soldiers who had escorted him left him at the foot of a wall, while the people of Orphalese began to gather in a circle around him, led by the Praxilas troop.

It must have been a terrible night for the boy. He seemed to have been beaten up, and no longer offered any resistance.

In the front row soon appeared the notables of Orphalese, led by Praxilas and Zain. The Aedile held his daughter firmly by the arm, for he knew his feelings for the condemned man. Tortured to see the man she loved treated in this way, she twisted her hands and wept tears.

The lieutenant who assisted Praxilas began to read the sentence :

"The man standing before you has been tried and found guilty of crimes against the city of Orphalese... Braving the martial law enacted to protect its inhabitants, he led a group of fanatical rebels to attack the city and spread terror and violence in its streets. Thanks to the courage of General Praxilas, the worst was averted and casualties were minimal. However, we cannot tolerate such unrest in the future."

The crowd began to stir. Soldiers were throwing blows

from all sides, so much tension was palpable, and the situation could degenerate at any moment.

"Let's get on with it," the officer said, sweeping the assembly with a metal-edged glance. "It is not our army that has suffered the greatest harm, but you, inhabitants of the noble Orphalese. So it is not we who must carry out the sentence, but you. We have come only at the request of the edile Zain, to ensure justice and security for all."

Suddenly, Yesmena pulled herself from her father's arms and rushed to Karim, facing the crowd to protect him.

"Leave him alone !" she shouted. "He's done nothing wrong ! Don't you see he's fighting for your freedom ?"

The inhabitants of Orphalese already felt very uncomfortable before this expeditious justice, but the irruption of the daughter of the edile disturbed them completely. Only Zain, wanting to enforce a semblance of order, stepped forward :

"Stay out of this, my daughter !" he said. "Karim has been found guilty of treason against his city."

"That's not true ! He has more courage than all of you ! He stands up to the invader, when all you do is bow down ! When someone tries to get in your way, you reach for your wrists... You'd stretch your neck if they wanted to slit your throat !"

Disconcerted by the attitude of his daughter, whose vehemence he discovered, Zain turned to the only recourse he seemed to have left. A bent and emaciated silhouette then painfully walked out of the rows, using a long cane to walk. He was the Venerable One of the temple, the supreme moral authority of Orphalese. The edile counted on his reputation for undisputed wisdom to bring everyone back to reason, and to make this authoritative decision accepted by invoking the Law.

The old man pointed a long skeletal finger at Yesmena :

"You're like Karim," said the old man, "your idealism blinds you !"

"That's normal, because we have the same fire in our veins ! That of love for our city ! And that of the love we feel for each other !"

Raising a chin full of challenge, she looked around the amazed assembly.

"Yes, I love this man," she said, pointing to Karim. "He represents the best of you, the future of your city ! That's why I gladly gave him my soul and my body !"

The Venerable One was stunned by this confession :

"What are you saying ?" he suffocated. "You gave yourself to this misbeliever ? You sacrificed your purity, this sacred jewel, outside the bonds of marriage ? And against beautiful words ? A curse on you !"

"And you, old man ! Who are you to tell me what to do ? By what right do you decree your truths ? By what authority do you rule our lives ?"

"From the right that I am the representative of God on earth ! And I command your punishment, sinner !"

"Your god does not exist, for he would never allow such injustice. You only represent your lust for power !"

The priest's eyes widened in disbelief at such an affront. Then he turned to the people, who were becoming increasingly agitated, and pointed to his victim :

"Stone her ! Stone them ! Punish this whore and her vicious lover ! Do you hear how they trampled on the Law ? Erase the filth that has caused all our evils ! For I tell you, I can explain better now the avalanche of our woes !"

The turmoil was at its height with this turnaround, and no one knew what to do. It was then that the captain made a signal that had been agreed upon with his men. A few stones began to fly. The first impacts were first heard on the wall, but as new throwers became more courageous, the blows soon became more accurate. Soon the first blood was spilled, unleashing the frenzy of the inhabitants. A shower of projectiles of all sizes began to fall on the young men.

Karim and Yesmena were hit on the head and collapsed. Most of the stones were now touching the bloody pile of flesh.

"Stop ! Stop it, you've gone insane !"

One man, alone, braving the murderous flood, had stepped forward to stop the slaughter. When the captain realized that it was General Praxilas himself, he ordered the soldiers to form ranks around their leader and point their spears at the inhabitants. The stoning ceased instantly.

Regardless of what was going on around him, he knelt down beside the girl and gently stroked her face. His coarse military fingers spread a bloody streak on the swollen forehead, which was still so delicate, so pure, just a moment ago. He looked for the pulse in the hollow of her neck.

When he straightened up, he was livid and visibly very affected. With a broken voice, he got mad at the assembly :

"The edile's daughter had nothing to do with this execution ! You're just a bunch of dumb monkeys !"

Then he looked up to the sky, his arms dangling, as if emptied of his substance.

The inhabitants looked at each other sideways, now aware that they had been the plaything of a fleeting madness. Those who still had a stone in their hands dropped it discreetly.

THE door of Youssef's cell opened suddenly, and in a great tumult four soldiers laid the lifeless body of the girl on the prisoner's mattress.

The old man could not help suppressing a cry when he saw her condition : she had been hit in many places, and her head was bleeding profusely. As he stood up, he saw Praxilas, who in turn entered the cramped room. But it was no longer the morgue-full general who had subdued so many cities. His eyes were haggard, he seemed completely lost.

A quick examination allowed Youssef to see the sinister truth : the teenager was dead.

"What have you done ? What happened ?" he asked the soldier in a white voice.

"I had nothing to do with it, it was she who intervened to save her lover, the rebel. The priests condemned her because she had sinned."

"She's crazy, and so are they ! You're all crazy !"

Tears began to run down his white beard.

"Tell me quickly, how is she ?" Praxilas inquired. "Did I intervene too late ?"

The old man shook his head negatively.

"There's nothing more to be done," he blew.

The general screamed in rage, clenching his fists, then fell to his knees. Slowly, he took Yesmena's hand.

"It is said that your prophet has called many souls back

from the realm of the dead," he breathed. "If he has given you the secret, do it for me, I beg you !"

The old man stroked his beard for a long time before answering.

"The Divine Consciousness alone decides who is to come back to life or not. It is not a benign act, for the departure of a being rarely comes at the wrong time in his personal history. I can pass on your request, but I cannot guarantee that it will be granted..."

"Yesmena's death cannot happen now, not this way !" shouted the general. "Resurrect her, I implore you ! I am lost without her !"

Youssef shook his head helplessly.

"The ways of life are mysterious," he says, "but they often depend on the purity of our intentions. If I were ever allowed to perform a miracle, if Yesmena were to come back to us, what would you do ? Would you leave this city ? Would you release all the prisoners ? Would you leave Orphalese in peace at last ?"

"I swear it ! My ship is repaired, and I have no reason to stay here. I will leave the city the way I found it."

The two men exchanged a look that sealed their agreement. Then the old man motioned for the general to leave :

"Leave me alone, for what is going to happen here cannot be seen with hostile eyes. I need serenity and silence."

Regretfully, the soldier slipped away, not without taking a last look at the little inert form that the disciple was now approaching.

Calm returned to the small room, and Youssef wondered what he was going to do. He had already witnessed many of the miracles Praxilas had spoken of, but he had never performed any himself. Almustafa said that it was a supreme act of faith, that it became a simple tool, a channel through which the divine will could be used as it wished.

The old man then placed his hands on the girl's body, one on her forehead and the other on her plexus, chanting a prayer that the Prophet had taught him, calling the divine conscience into him and abandoning all personal desires.

He began to repeat this prayer again and again, swinging mechanically back and forth, and gradually plunging into a hypnotic sleep. He lost all notion of time, forgetting his doubts and fear of failure, forgetting himself.

The city once called Orphalese disappeared and became no place.

The man once called Youssef disappeared and became no one, just a conduit for a mysterious external will.

An infinite amount of time passed thus, far from men and their conflicts, and as if outside the world. Youssef did not move his hands, but he did not tire. He felt torrents of energy running down his arms, hands and fingers, to flood Yesmena's lifeless limbs.

*

* *

At one point, an imperceptible breath seemed to animate the blue lips, and a wave of heat ran under the icy skin. Yesmena fluttered her eyelids, then opened her eyes, as if surprised at what was happening to her.

Lost in gratitude when he realized what had just happened, Youssef smiled broadly and kissed her slender little fingers, as if to prevent her from leaving again.

"Thank you for showing me the way, O Master !" he simply articulated, his cheeks bathed in tears. And he thought that, truly, the mysteries of Life were unfathomable...

*

* *

Praxilas had been pacing around for hours in the guards' room of the prison, with a pale complexion and a tortured soul. Yes, he obviously loved this girl more than he could have said himself. Yes, the bloodthirsty brute that he was was disarmed by her passing. The sacrifice of the young innocent girl would have made him laugh just a week earlier, and now he was petrified of it. The object of his desires had shown such purity, such self-denial in love, that it opened under his feet like an abyss of unknown feelings.

Then, the flabbergasted general suddenly saw the frail figure of Yesmena stepping forward into the doorway. Cadaveric, bloody, staggering at every step, but alive ! And beautiful, so beautiful...

Praxilas threw himself to the ground, crying :

"Thank you, Lord ! O thank you ! You are my Creator and I am your humble servant !"

He kissed the girl's feet, wetting them with his tears, but she pushed him away sharply :

"Let us in peace, my city and me ! Leave with your soldiers, and never come back. Teenager-man, who only conceives of power and violence ! Wolf-man, who preys on his own brothers ! May Orphalese remain forever outside your dreams of conquest, you and your fellow fools !"

The frail young girl was no longer recognizable, and she expressed herself like a queen. In truth, she looked more like a goddess who had returned from the Inferno to give her imperious orders.

Like a child caught at fault being lectured, Praxilas stood up and nodded silently. He still wanted to tell her that he adored her, that he wanted to take her with him, but Youssef appeared behind her, coming out of the shadows, and it was as if the ghost of Almustafa himself came back to haunt him, reproaching him for the incalculable sum of his mistakes.

Defeated, overwhelmed by the miracle he had just witnessed, he left the prison without a word.

S EVERAL days had passed since the stoning of Karim
and the resurrection of Yesmena, and Praxilas had
not been seen again. Even his second in command had no
news, and did not know where he could hide.

The general had changed. He no longer wore his uni-
form of purple and gold, but a simple soldier's tunic. He
was no longer shaving, and his hair looked as if it had
suddenly turned white since the miracle. He spent his days
in Youssef's hut, listening to stories about Almustafa. He
knew the whole town was hostile to his presence, and
with the ship repaired, he could no longer delay his departure. So he had very little time to immerse himself in
the teachings of the Beloved, for whom he had suddenly
discovered a passion.

At first, the disciple had been reluctant to share his
knowledge with this lifelong enemy, who had hunted down
and killed so many of his friends over the past two decades.
But he agreed to listen to the story of Praxilas. The general
spoke at length about him, as he had never done before.
He hoped that this preamble, without absolving his faults,
would perhaps allow him to justify his past actions, and
would open the disciple's confidence. And it was like a
confession, pronounced slowly, in a low voice, his gaze
obstinately lowered to the ground.

"I come from a poor rural family," he began. "But I've

always been full of ambition, and I reached the nearest big city as soon as I could. The military career was the ideal way for me to make my way in the world and erase the traces of my lowly extraction. Indeed, our empire is greedy, in perpetual expansion, and I quickly understood that I had a gift for command, which would serve me, from victory to conquest, to make a name for myself, and to rise quickly in the hierarchy and society. I thus became the instrument of the empire, satiating it with its appetite for new territories, but never for long.

"I was still very young when I crossed the road to Almustafa. I was indeed barely twenty-five years old when I received my first command as a general, and I was, I must confess, very nervous and anxious to have for the first time several thousand men under my command.

"Was I overwhelmed by the magnitude of the task? Well, perhaps... I was looking for a way to assert my authority over the troops.

"Was it our destiny? Were we the playthings of forces that were beyond us? Anyway, the Almustafa affair came at just the right time to serve my plans.

"We had heard about this strange man, whom some people called a prophet, even in the capital, and as more and more people followed him, I was asked to investigate him, and to act according to what I discovered...

"Our nation has never held priests and gods in high esteem. We use them when necessary to pacify conquered peoples, but as you have seen, I am a radical atheist. Our empire, since its foundation, has been built on the progress of reason and science. It is our scientists who have given us our military superiority and the comfort in our cities that all foreign nations envy us. Until very recently, and much more so at the time, I therefore considered everything that resembled a religion to be a sectarian embrace, a poison

136

that drives people mad.

"Therefore, even as I lurked around watching him, I never paid attention to what Almustafa was saying. If I was struck by the size of the crowds that came to listen to him, not for a second did I imagine that something extraordinary could happen during these gatherings. I pitied those poor buggers who were being fooled by a self-centred, power-hungry manipulator, who certainly had charisma and oratory skills, but no direct connection with any deity.

"However, the multitudes were growing around him at the same time as his aura among the people, and I saw the moment coming when such displacements of people could not go smoothly with the local villagers, because between two public meetings, all these people far from home were looking for something to eat and nooks and crannies to sleep in, without necessarily having the means to do so, and without the regions they were passing through being able to accommodate so many people !

"When the first orchards were ransacked and the first farms plundered, I tell myself that we had come to the breaking point, at the same time as the glory of the Prophet. The time had come for me to put an end to his legend. If I could do so, what a resounding success it would be ! My reputation would be made !

"It was easy for us to infiltrate these disparate groups, and to provoke clashes, dissension and violence on the fringes of the gatherings. Soon, political demands, calls for the liberation of our yoke, circulated in the presence of your Master, amalgamating, then substituting for his words of peace.

"It was then only a matter of days before sufficiently serious disturbances broke out and required the intervention of my troops to restore order. The seditious, known to all, was implicitly designated, and I myself arrested Almustafa with the consent of my hierarchy and all the potentates of the region, who saw in a bad light the growing popularity of this barefoot who questioned their very legitimacy, in addition to sowing disorder.

"The court in charge of judging him was sympathetic to our cause, and quickly sentenced him to be stoned to death for calling for resistance and revolt against our forces.

"Today, I understand the extent of my mistake, which can never be undone. My foolishness has robbed the world of a great opportunity for truth, wisdom and enlightenment such as it has never known before.

"I am beyond forgiveness, I know this and do not ask you for it. But I can try to lessen the impact of my faults : I want to spend the rest of my days transmitting the light that I have tried to extinguish. Tell me what I must do to become a disciple of the Beloved too !Teach me !"

Youssef listened to the story of Praxilas without saying a word, thinking that if he had been twenty years younger, he would certainly have jumped down his throat. He couldn't believe that he was facing the man he had hated most in his whole life, the man who had killed his dreams along with his mentor, annihilating his hopes of a humanity revived by a radically new vision of spirituality.

The old man took time to digest everything he had heard, and to find the right course of action. But as always when he was in the grip of anger and doubt, he wondered what the Prophet would have done in such a case. Of course, Almustafa would have rejected no one, even if he had been his executioner. He would have taken the time and smiled the necessary smiles and found the right words. His interlocutors, whom he would have treated the same regardless of their origin, would have left enlightened, appeased, and filled with a new vision of hope in the world.

He contemplated the large carcass that was weeping its eyes out, and it was like a dam that had just given way, a hand stretched out that could not fail to be grasped...

FOR the next few days, the old disciple tried to inculcate in the general the broad outlines of his master's vision of life, human consciousness, the oneness of all that is, the need to go beyond appearances to reach the invisible reality that underlies the visible...

It was of course an impossible task in such a short time, but Praxilas' thirst seemed unquenchable, and he systematically acquiesced to everything he received. As a young child discovering the world, he kept asking questions about the mysteries of the universe :

"Why do we die ? And why are there so many massacres ? Why does the divine conscience sacrifice so many of its creatures ?" the soldier asked, for example.

"See how nature puts everything on numbers," replied the old man. "She throws thousands of offspring into the unknown so that a few may come of age and reproduce, perpetuating their race. Look at all her abortive attempts to make one work at last, more fortunate or more suitable. See how some species are modified by their environment to live, survive again and again, and bring consciousness to the most hostile places !

"Life is an infinite ocean, pushing its waves relentlessly into the world for them to discover it, and for them to know themselves as they discover it.

"Of course, in this incessant surf, whole generations of creatures are born and disappear in every imaginable way. But when they die and leave their material envelope, the consciousness that animated them returns to the great reserve of the One Consciousness, to participate in the next wave, in the next generations of creatures, again and again, each time with a little more knowledge and love for all that is !

"All these trials and sufferings that we are going through are not necessary, they only exist because we have forgotten that we are all co-creators of the universe. They are only there to help us recover our memory. But we take so many lives to understand, we are capable of repeating the same mistakes so many times..."

or else :
"Why is there war ? Who has sown this seed of discord in our hearts ?"

"You're naturally afraid of what you don't know. And what you fear, you try to destroy, so you won't be afraid anymore. We're here on Earth to discover how to overcome that primal reflex... We must learn to love those whose opinions differ from our own. We must learn that difference brings thought to life. We have only one common goal, and that is the realization of the human soul, of the divine within us, through unconditional acceptance of the other, and through increasing our knowledge of each other, which leads to freedom, compassion, creativity.

"You and your enemy are like the left and right hand of the same body, which would have put on different coloured gloves. All your life you don't care what colour the other's glove is, one is leather, the other is wool, one is discarded, the other is a mitt, how laughable ! You insult each other, you fight, you try to eliminate each other by all means.

"But one day you leave this material world and join the universal consciousness, leaving the skin of the gloves behind you. At last you see yourself as you are, identical in every way, and part of the same great perfect body !

"Then you kiss each other laughing and exclaim : what a beautiful comedy we have played in this wonderful theatre designed for us ! What part do you want to play next time ?

"Most people think that they are just gloves that are thrown away at the end of existence because they have become unusable. They despair of that ; they have forgotten that they are the hand, which takes turns using multiple gloves according to the know-how, the know-how that it wants to perfect !"

Taken by the fire of his explanations, Youssef suddenly had an idea. He grasped the pieces of crockery he had bought from Alhéna and Munir just a few weeks ago, and it seemed like an eternity.

He brandished a cup and a plate in front of the general :

"The divine will is the potter ; consciousness is the clay ; the human ego is the shape of the modeled object, which makes the cup say : *I am a cup, not a plate !*

"You're a cup, Praxilas, and so far you've hated plates. From now on, you must think first and foremost that you are clay, and that everything around you is made of the same clay as you are, absolutely everything : other men whatever their origin, animals, plants, minerals, the Earth, the planets, the stars... absolutely everything !

"The whole universe, meaning God, meaning Life, is just a big block of clay that is constantly projected in temporary forms to know itself !"

Stunned, the general rubbed his temples with his eyes wide open, trying to grasp a few snippets of what was being said to him...

THE young Mustapha climbed the raid that led to Youssef's hut with nervousness and anxiety, which was not like him.

Since the night when he and his gang of friends had diverted Almitra's departure from the city, he had had to live without his reassuring presence for the first time. So he had spent several days alone, taking care of his grandmother Nedjma, and it seemed that these trials, these new responsibilities, by bringing the inane world of adults brutally into his childlike mind, had suddenly matured him. His features had hardened, and he seemed even taller, almost a teenager already, with a serious look, full of new understandings.

During the revolt and the street fighting he had tried to protect the house by sealing the openings with what he could find, barricading the door with a pile of furniture. In the end, all these precautions had proved useless, for the violence of the battle had never approached their neighbourhood, and had only cost them a few hours of anguish and uncertainty.

Then his mother had finally been able to return to Orphalossa, thanks to the general disorder that had followed Karim's execution, and she had immediately taken matters into her own hands. Returning from the mountain with other fugitives who had given up any desire to fight, she had noticed the traces left by the assaults, both on the facades and in the minds and bodies of people. She had seen the marks left by the assaults, both on the facades and in the minds and bodies of those who had been killed, but also the wounded, who needed urgent attention. Those who had not been taken in by their families had been gathered together in a few public buildings, and particularly in the Temple, which intended to restore its reputation tarnished by the more than questionable attitude of the Venerable.

In the meantime, in order to calm the situation, and in the absence of Praxilas, about whom there had been no news since the "miracle", the foreign troops had been discreet, and had concentrated their efforts on putting their ship back in the water and preparing for departure as soon as possible. We were now waiting for the return of the General-in-Chief to weigh anchor.

Arriving in front of the house, the child saw the disciple sitting on the doorstep, in great conversation with a stranger with a sad expression on his face. The two men stopped as he approached.

"Hey, my friend Mustapha," said Youssef with a big smile. "What have you come all the way here for ?"

"My mother is well, if you are interested," replied the child with a reproachful look. "She is with the doctors and priests, overwhelmed by the number of victims, and has sent me to fetch you because your help would be more than welcome ! Where have you been then ? Why did you leave us when we need you most ?"

"I met a soul in distress, who took me," said an embarrassed Youssef. "I introduce you to General Praxilas, who is the cause of all the torments of the city..."

Despite this unflattering presentation, the soldier offered a friendly hand to the young boy in an attempt to initiate contact, but Mustapha did not flinch.

146

"You too are eagerly awaited," he said simply, crossing his arms. "Your ship is back in the harbour, and only you are missing. It seems to me that the time of your departure has already been delayed too much."

Praxilas then gave the old man a look which, to Mustapha's great surprise, seemed to be tinged with despair. But what had happened between those two ? What had they told each other ?

"The boy is right," admitted Youssef. "If you stay longer, more violence will break out, and you won't have the advantage this time. It's better for everyone if we stay here."

The men got up, and the older one leaning on the child's shoulder because of his aching legs, the strange little group slowly set off back down to the town.

THE vessel had left the refit dock and was floating lazily in Orphalese harbour, ready to go. There were still many marks of the fighting she had had against the elements, but she looked much better than when she arrived, and could return to her home port safely. Enemy sailors and soldiers were all aboard, waiting for their general to finally join them and cast off.

As they were about to embark, Praxilas took Youssef's arm, and his voice trembled when he said :

"Master, I don't know how to thank you... You have given meaning to my life."

The old man made an annoying gesture :

"Don't call me master, for I've been repeating someone else's words to you. And don't thank me either, I only shared my ignorance with you !"

"But I feel lost now. I was a beast, I fed only on blood, and here I am like a little child who has just been born and sees the world with new eyes. Tell me again, what shall I do now ?"

"You want to change the world ? Spread Almustafa's message of wisdom and light everywhere ? Then just change your way of seeing things. It is your thoughts that create everything you experience, and the world is only the sum of the aspirations and fears of all the creatures in it. If you want the best to happen, remove fear and exclusion from your mind ; make sure that everything that comes out of you, your gestures, your words, and even your innermost desires, are always of the highest order. For everything that goes from you goes towards what surrounds you, colours and modifies it, and then returns to you as an echo, in the form of good or bad things, according to what you have generated...

"Do you want to do good ? Then live in your flesh that the Divine Consciousness permeates everything, and that consequently, It is the innate good in everything. The very essence of goodness is to be truly united with everything in knowledge, love and service..."

The warrior looked at Youssef with the empty eyes of one who did not understand. The old man put his hand on the strong shoulder with compassion, as a father blesses an unworthy son who leaves home for good. Then some words of the Prophet came back to him, and he pronounced them aloud :

"To the hungry, give bread.
For bread is his god.

To the thirsty, give water
For water is his goddess.

To the unfortunate, make him smile
For joy is his hope.

To the unloved, give your friendship
For it is his inaccessible treasure.

To the sick, give health
Because it's like candlelight
The only guide in the depths of his night.

150

Truly, I'm telling you : He's not ready to hear
        the chant of the world
The one who's not satiated
Of his own gods.

Then give with faith.
Give with humility.
Share with dignity.
Share with joy !"

*

* *

When the lieutenant welcomed his chief on board, he
had difficulty recognizing him. He hadn't seen him for several days, and could not suspect the inner revolutions he
was going through. After greeting him as is customary in
the military, the officer could not help but make a disapproving pout. Turning around on the platform, he discovered
a scene that left him stunned.

That the disciple of Almustafa was present to celebrate
the departure of his sworn enemy was understandable, but
that he greeted him with a serene smile and a mark of peace
and affection was beyond comprehension. The lieutenant
crossed the old man's gaze for a moment, and trembled at
his bases. How could such strength emanate from such a
frail being, so close to the tomb ? What strange powers did
he possess that so easily turned the war dog Praxilas into a
combat-unfit wreck ?

It wasn't until the silhouette of the refurbished ship
vanished on the horizon that all the people of Orphalese

could loudly burst into joy, the happiness of peace and freedom, even though they knew it would take a long time to heal the wounds, for many families mourned the young people lost in battle.

Youssef, however, remained perplexed. He had just let go a man who was going to repeat what he had understood from the words of the Prophet. He too would henceforth be considered a disciple of the Beloved, but a disciple who had hardly known the man, and who in any case had not been chosen by him, had never lived with him. As he thoughtfully stroked his white beard, the eternal wanderer wondered what his teachings, barely sketched out, might well become in the mouth of his former torturer...

Epilogue

PRAXILAS and his army had been gone for nearly three weeks, and Yesmena was slowly recovering from his wounds, along with the city of Orphalese. The last rebels who had taken refuge in the mountains had now all returned to the city, and were helping to rebuild it.

On the advice of Youssef, the edile's daughter had settled with Almitra, whose science of ointments, healing oils and herbs was known to all, and would help the miraculous woman to recover her health.

The disciple also hoped that the long conversations between the two women would gradually erase the trauma of the loss of Karim, her lover put to death under the horrible conditions of stoning.

Every day, Almitra brought the news to her patient. They always contained their share of surprises, because Orphalese's face changed quickly, in reaction to the dramatic events that the city had just gone through.

Thus, as soon as the dark enemy ship had disappeared from view, the anger of the crowd turned against the edile Zain, whose militia had participated in the massacre of the rebellious youth, and whose submission to the enemy's will had become evident during the public execution.

The inhabitants felt guilty, of course, that they had allowed themselves to be drawn into this madness, but the general feeling was that they had been fooled by the Aedile and the Venerable, who had confused their minds, so that they were not really responsible for their actions.

In the opinion of all, after what had happened, Zain could not remain the edile of the city. Suddenly it was realized that he had been in the job for several decades, and that the time for change had come. They formed groups that searched tirelessly for him to push him to resign, even to hold him accountable *manu militari*, by searching the city street by street, house by house. But after several days, Zain was still nowhere to be found. The bad tongues claimed that to escape his fate, he had fled into the mountains, taking the place of the rebels he had helped to fight.

The most vindictive, whose hot-tempered spirits did not subside, suggested that his house be taken over and plundered in retaliation. The wrath of those who entered the imposing building was only magnified by the accumulation of wealth they discovered there. Precious objects, tapestries, fine crockery, luxury furniture, everything breathed the greatest ease, and a comfort to which no inhabitant had ever had access ! No, the edile Zain was definitely not the cantor of virtue that they thought they had chosen, and the systematic ransacking of every room in the house barely satisfied their thirst for justice.

By order of the city council, the militia was disbanded, and a vote was taken to replace it with a police force based on the conscription of the city's young boys when they reached the age of majority, for a period of one year, renewable if necessary, financed no longer by the fortunes of a few wealthy landlords, but by the taxes of all the inhabitants.

At the same time, a drama had unfolded in the temple, unbeknownst to all : a novice had discovered the Venerable's lifeless body in his bed, bathed in a pool of blood. It is said that the weight of remorse had become unbearable, and that he had preferred to open his veins rather than face the gaze of his parishioners. Led by his aging hand, the conduct of the Temple with the occupanhad been more than open to criticism, and the last followers of The Law were deserting its colonnades.

However, despite the anger aroused by her father, Yesmena had become a popular heroine because she did not hesitate to put her life in danger out of love. After the miracle she had enjoyed, followed by the departure of the occupiers, she was now almost considered a saint, to whom the inhabitants attributed the liberation of the city. In addition, the tragic end of her story with Karim was the subject of much conversation and legend ; the words she had said to herself just before the execution were repeated, and her attitude was praised for the nobility and self-sacrifice that Zain lacked.

So much so that one fine morning Almitra stormed into the girl's room :

"The City Council is planning a party in your honor in a few days, as soon as you've fully recovered !" she announced triumphantly, certain that it would put some balm in her patient's heart.

Yesmena twisted her nose, as if disgusted at the thought of having to go back into the world again.

"I really don't have the spirit for celebrations," she said wearily.

"I understand you, and it will be difficult at first, no doubt," Almitra replied. "But you'll have to get out sometime, or else you'll sink into a deadly depression from which you won't be able to get out !"

The convalescent nodded unwillingly.

"I've had time to think, during all these days of inaction," she replied, "and an idea has crossed my mind. A woman has never been edile of Orphalese, but mentalities change. I'm sure the Council would be willing to let me have the keys to the municipal palace, because of my sudden fame, and the political renown of my family. But I'm still only a child, and I'm not cut out for this role. However, if the time for women has come, we must not let it pass, and you would be a perfect candidate !"

Almitra couldn't help puffing, as this proposal seemed so absurd to her. But the girl did not smile, and continued to stare at her with her penetrating gaze, which could become disturbing in the long run :

"Don't you have enough experience in the affairs of the city ? And aren't you appreciated by everyone ? You alone would command the respect of the entire Council to carry out the reforms necessary for the city's evolution, in peace, fairness, and listening to everyone ! Don't you think we need a long period of serenity ?"

Then the former seer of the temple realized that this was no joke, and frowned to show the utmost seriousness.

"I'll think about it..." she finally promised.

"Rise up, women," suddenly cried the old Nedjma across the room, "and take the world back from the hands of men, who have led it into wandering and chaos !"

Yesmena and Almitra looked at each other, taken aback, and then burst out laughing. What if the ancestor, in the end, didn't lose a crumb of what was going on under her roof ?

*

* *

The child and the old man watched the ocean break on the rocks below. Sitting next to each other on the edge of the cliff, they were rocked by the soft, deep rumbling of the surf.

Mustapha put his hand on the disciple's arm, as a sign of affection, and looked him in the eyes :

"How many pages have you written about the life of the Prophet, and how many pages have you transcribed ?"

"Alas, not a word yet ! I don't know how to begin. I suppose I'm overwhelmed by the enormity of the task..."

"It's better this way, I think. His parables were traced in the sand. Let the wind blow them away and the sea erase them. So they will not be frozen, or worse, distorted by the languor of centuries to come."

The white-bearded man looked at the kid, frowning :

"Who are you, young sprout, to utter such nonsense ?"

But the child continued on his way :

"Truly, Youssef, my brother, beyond boundless spaces, a mother carried me again. I am back !"

"What do you say ?"

"Were you looking for a ghost when you came to this city where I once lived ? Did you want to dig up a corpse ? Didn't you know in your heart that I was well alive ?"

Incredulous, Youssef looked into the child's eyes for a long time. And he knew that in truth, the Prophet had returned. He could not contain his tears as he embraced the boy.

Cover design :
Les Eclosions Asynchrones Studio

ISBN 978-2-9556679-4-1